Abaddon

Abaddon

<u>A Novel</u>

By Edward Bowers

Abaddon

This is a work of fiction. Names, characters, businesses, events, and incidents are the product of the author's imagination. Any resemblance to actual persons, living or dead, or actual events is purely coincidental.

Copyright © Edward Bowers, 2024
All rights reserved.
The moral rights of the author have been asserted.

No part of this book may be reproduced in any form on by any electronic or mechanical means, including information storage and retrieval systems, without permission in writing from the publisher, except by a reviewer who may quote brief passages in review.

Written by: Edward Bowers
Cover image created by: Jennifer Rudisuhle
Editing by: Jennifer Rudisuhle and Rachel Shores

Abaddon

Abaddon

Abaddon

*I dedicate this book to my closest friend, Jen.
You are more influential and inspiring than you will ever know.
You are a beautiful and strong person.
I am glad to have you in my life and wish you the best.
Thank you for all your input and help.*

Abaddon

Abaddon

Contents
Intro…9
Chapter 1…13
Chapter 2…21
Chapter 3…31
Chapter 4…37
Chapter 5…45
Chapter 6…59
Chapter 7…73
Chapter 8…77
Chapter 9…83
Chapter 10…89
Chapter 11…95
Chapter 12…103
Chapter 13…109
Chapter 14…113
Chapter 15…121
Chapter 16…131
Chapter 17…145
Chapter 18…153
Chapter 19…165
Chapter 20…171
Outro…177
Acknowledgment…181

Abaddon

Abaddon

Intro

Hello. I am Abaddon, a being whose origins are shrouded in mystery. I bring you a tale that may initially seem insignificant, but it is a narrative that transcends the realms of belief. This story could have led to a living hell on earth. Yet, it all changed with the arrival of a man named John.

But first, allow me to introduce myself. Heaven created me, but I also came from hell—a creation that was viewed as both good and evil. Some of you might know me better as the Angel of Death or the one who brought on the bugs in Egypt for Moses. I have spent thousands of years carrying souls to heaven or hell. I was a heartless, emotionless entity with a job to do until I met a human named John. I have always been good with the job God gave me; I did it well. But this man, this human John, changed me.

I am cursed by my mother and may not be able to fulfill my destiny, what God created me to do. This may not seem like much to you, but if it were not for John and his unwavering love, I would never have the hope to do what is needed of me. He was a good man, a loving man. Love is not an emotion we angels have, but not that kind of love. Not the type John had for Caroline. The strength he had was insurmountable. He was the second man I know of to actually walk through hell for the woman he loved. I have met many men who claim to be willing to do such a thing but never take that task on, yet he did, simply out of love. That kind of love that can move mountains and change destinies should never be let go of. It should be held onto and cherished.

Abaddon

My existence was once straightforward, a mere instrument of divine will. But then, I crossed paths with John, and his love for another ignited a fire within me. A conflict, a struggle, began to brew, challenging the very core of my being, my purpose. The path ahead was uncertain, filled with obstacles I had never anticipated.

Then, I found myself confined within a human body. This hindered my ability to fulfill my duties and opened my eyes to the concept of right and wrong. I realized my mother's actions were unjust, and I was determined to make her cease or face the consequences. Trapped in this immense power and vulnerability paradox, I desperately needed assistance. This predicament, this duality, is something I wouldn't wish upon anyone. The feeling of vulnerability, of being at the mercy of others, is something I want you to understand, to feel with me.

I have heard many men talk about doing anything for the women they love just to prove it to anyone. Some have said they would walk through heaven and hell to prove their love, but never would. But not John; he took on that challenge. He did it for the love of his wife and made it through.

I enlisted John's help to join me against a common enemy and to help release me of this curse, to free my prince, my soul, so I could move forward and be there for God's plan on Judgement Day. This is part of my story, that part that was supposed to free me. I had all the hope in the world to be freed. But not everyone's plan turns out the way they had hoped. You may be left with unanswered questions, but isn't that life as we know it?

God works in mysterious ways, does he not? I am here to tell my story of why I needed a man's help to get back to being there for God.

Abaddon

Abaddon

Abaddon

Chapter 1

Abaddon is a Hebrew name that means "destroyer." Also known as the Angel of Death.

The room was a realm of shadows, the only glimmer of light emanating from the flickering fire. It was an ancient house, its age etched into the worn wooden beams and the creaking floorboards. Yet, it had been lovingly restored, not to a modern standard, but to a more authentic, original state. With its expansive rooms, the house seemed too grand for a solitary dweller. No other lights illuminated the darkness, the fire's dance casting eerie shapes on the walls. As she crossed the threshold, I, Abaddon, the Angel of Death, materialized to greet her, adding to the sense of ancient mystery that hung in the air.

"Greetings and welcome. You must be Paige." A deep and resonant voice, its source concealed in the shadows, echoed from the living room, adding to the air of mystery that enveloped the house. Though warm, the voice held a hint of something more that made Paige's heart skip a beat.
"Yes, my name is Paige. The note on the door said to come in." Paige responded to the voice.
"Please come in and warm yourself by the fire. I love fires. They remind me of home. Come sit down by the fire. Dry off. The storms are bad tonight. You must be cold. Would you like a drink?"
"Thank you."

Abaddon

Paige exuded a sense of casual cool in a black hoody, jeans, and black canvas tennis shoes. Her attire, reminiscent of a bygone era, hinted at a past as mysterious as the house she had entered. She walked over to the couch and sat down; she placed her computer bag and purse next to her. The couch was an older red couch with wood trimming around the back, which was very uncomfortable, something you might see in an old Victorian house. Paige settled in as if she would be there for a while. She reached into her purse, pulled out a voice recorder, and placed it on the coffee table before her.

She was in awe of the man who sat in the chair before her. His chiseled features and long black hair brushed the tops of his shoulders. As she examined him, she could not find a flaw in him. His skin was perfectly tanned, which was odd in Paige's mind as it was not summer. How was he tanned, she wondered? She noticed a scar on his cheek and hands from the fire's flickering light. His nails were long and black.

"What is it you are looking for, Paige?"
"You called me and said you had a story to tell. I'm here to record that story for you." She responded confidently.
"And write it?"
"If that is what you want."
"That is pleasing."
"Ok, let us begin, shall we? Tell me your name."
"Well, my mother called me Brad; I hated that name. It was not me. I am Abaddon."
"So, you are a demon? Abaddon, isn't Satan afraid of you? Aren't you a little small to be Abaddon?"
"What do you mean small? Why all these questions?"

Abaddon

"I need answers so that I can write this book for you."
"Then let me tell you the story. I have a lot to say, and if you keep asking these damned questions, we will never get anywhere."
"Ok, so you are Abaddon, got it. Go on."
"Yes, I am a demon born out of hate. But this is not my first time on earth. But this is my longest time on earth. I have never had a mother; I have just manifested here. I never had a mother before; this was new to me."

Paige was listening intently to Abaddon and his story as it began. The storm outside was weakening, and the rain was stopping. The recorder could record for hours, and it did not use cassette tapes, so Paige did not have to worry about making him stop and start so she could switch tapes.

"I chose you, Paige, because of your writing. You do not report on the usual daily interactions of this world. You may not be the best writer in the business, but I find your blog to be very informative on the demonic. It's very accurate for a human. But you miss some points. I hope I can help you fill in some blanks for your readers."
"I miss some points. Like what?" She asked him.
"I will get to those points in a few, but I have struggled over the years as a human, not as a demon. It disgusts me to be in this human body, and I am feeling stuck."
"Ok, go on."

15

Abaddon

"I don't know where to start. Should I start with him, my mother, definitely not from when I first came to earth?"
"Start wherever; I have plenty of room to record. We have plenty of time; I know I arrived a little late, but it is only seven o'clock."
"Very well, I can give some background, but I will start with my mother and him."

He began his story by ensuring Paige recorded and listened to him and what he told her. She needed to understand, not just record and write.

"As I said, my name is Abaddon. I am one of Hell's demons, yet at the same time, I am one of Heaven's angels. I am in command of the sixth house of hell. I am both from Heaven and hell. Most Christians know I am the 'Angle of the Abyss.' The Bible does not speak of me correctly; I am an enigma or a mystery to most. I am not the large, humanoid figure with locust-like futures I am generally described as. I do not have a herd of bugs following me, but I can summon them as needed. I do not have the features of a locust myself, but I can manifest that form if you would like."
"No, no need for that. I am not a bug person myself."
"I have gone by several names over the years before my mother had me. See, before I was made in this human body by her, I was called Abaddon or Apollyon, even "the Angel of Death." At one point, I was named Muriel and charged by God himself to collect from the earth to be used in the creation of Adam. I was even appointed as his guardian before

Abaddon

my fall. Before my fall, everyone, including the angels, demons, and mortal creatures, felt fear of me due to my size. My appearance has often been described as 'overwhelmingly' frightening, and my mere presence would destroy spirits 'through their own screams.' Moses even called me to cause the great rains during the ten plagues of Egypt. I was even mentioned in Enoch's writings. You know, one of the many books the church took out of the Bible?"
"I know of the book of Enoch. You were mentioned in that book?"
"Yes, I was. I had been appointed as the warden of Sheol, where I guarded the desolate and hellish prison of the treacherous 'Watchers.' Alternatively, however, I was also the warden of Tartus and the prince of Tartaruchi. I remember being present at the tomb of Jesus at the exact moment he was resurrected. Again, I tell you that I am an enigma, with heaven and hell claiming me as their ally and, at other times, an enemy. To be considered the 'Angel of Death and Destruction', the demon of the abyss, as well as being known as the true king of all demons. Yes, I Regret to say that some believe that I reign over Satan or Lucifer himself. I have even been known to be in league with Satan, even going as far as to claim that I may be Satan. A name I am not sure I want to be attached to me. He is a separate entity from myself. I have been sent to cast Satan down to the abyss and seal him when the time comes. When God says, it is time for the End of Days. I have been given a particular role from God regarding the 'Last Day of Judgement.' As I will be taking the souls to the Valley of Josaphat. Due to my vast power, some have even

Abaddon

prayed to me for a chance of being saved. Even as big and powerful as Satan is, he avoids any confrontation with me. Making people think I am more dangerous than the King of Hell."

"Is it true that it has been prophesied that you will command a monstrous horde from the Abyss as the Locust of Abaddon that will rampage over the earth in the tribulation period as Judgement Day approaches?" Paige interrupted.

"That is what they say, yes. The horde will be prohibited from killing any living creature by God once they have given the Seam of Lord but will torment the impure for five months, and the torture will be so horrible that mankind will try to kill themselves, but death will avoid them. It is I who will be opening the gates of the great abyss to unleash upon this earth the swarms of demons and locusts, who will then proceed to torture those of mankind who do not bear the mark or seal of God upon their forehead. After that, I am to seize Satan himself, bind him, and toss him into the bottomless pit for a thousand years." He boasted. *"But I am not here to tell you about my future duties to the Lord."*

"What are we here to talk about, then?"

"We are here to talk about my mother and the devastation she brought on her ex-husband and the curse she put on me. The one I need to be released from so I can do what I must do when the Day of Judgment comes. But you need that bit of history to understand."

Paige realized this would be a long night for her and Abaddon. She got comfortable and pulled out a pad of paper

Abaddon

and pen; she was still recording every word of his but also wanted to write things down.

> *"Then let's continue."*
> *"Let's."*
> *"What shall I call you?"*
> *"Write me as Abaddon; that will be fine."*
> *"So, tell me. Why me? Why you? Tell me everything."*
> *"My dear Paige. I can't just tell you everything at once. It will take me some time to get to all the points and answer your questions. But why me? Well, I have never been in a problem like this before. I have already told you about me. But why? If I cannot get out of this human body in time, I will not be here to do what God wants or needs me to do for him at the end of time. As I stated before, I am to cast Satan into the great abyss. I can only do that if I am back in my original form. I have been cursed to this body you see before yourself. I hope that by telling you this story and posting it, someone will see and be able to do something. Maybe someone will be able to break this curse of mine. But let's start my story. Maybe from here, your answers will come. It was about three years ago I was born; well, this body was born. And a year ago, Satan tricked me and cursed me by locking my essence in this body. A year ago, that Mother ordered me and the others to break his heart again. A year ago, that Mother ordered us to take her away from him. I have not seen him now for six months. Six long months since their love for each other changed me."*
> *"Okay, so I am supposed to post your story so you can get some help?"*

Abaddon

"You are going to post my story to prepare people for the day of the Lord's return, Judgement Day."

Abaddon continued with his story.

Chapter 2

It was three years ago. He was a single man—well, a divorced man—easy on the eyes to some. He was of average height, standing about 5'11" with a toned athletic physique, but he did work out to ensure he kept it. His piercing blue eyes were the one thing most people noticed about him. It always made him feel awkward with the attention they drew from others. His mom would say that besides his kindness and compassion, his best attribute was his eyes. Underneath his confident exterior, he was a man who had experienced deep love and heartbreak, and this vulnerability, this rawness, made him relatable. This vulnerability, so often hidden, made him open to the possibility of a new love, a new beginning.

He knew he was no supermodel, but he was not the ugliest man on the planet. It had been years since he had been with anyone. Ever since his last divorce, he had decided to focus on himself and his kids. He had never anticipated meeting a woman like her with such beauty. It was more her soul and heart that he was attracted to than her outer beauty. But her outer beauty was not a bad thing to him either. He felt like the luckiest man when she started talking with him. It happened so fast for him—a man who had cut off all hopes and dreams of ever finding a woman again. His anticipation and hope for a new beginning were palpable, making the audience share his joy and his newfound hope. A love came unexpectedly, like a sweet surprise in his life.

She never thought of herself as a beautiful woman, not that she thought she was ugly. They were a good-looking couple together. But his love for her was beyond physical beauty. It was a love that knew no bounds and consumed him. She meant the world to him. He thought about her every minute of every day. He dreamed of the day he could move to be with her. He knew it would be a while, but he started planning and saving for the day. His love never wavered for her, even after she left the relationship. In his eyes, she was indeed perfection for him. But to him, she was the most beautiful person on earth, and his love for her, his unwavering devotion, was a force to be reckoned with.

One of the things he loved about her was her height. She was not short or tall; to him, she was above average for a lady. To him, she was the perfect height. There was little to complain about when it came to her.

From the start, he had feared that she would leave him; he feared that he would be unable to make it work. He had always done something to mess relationships up in the past. But they had never understood him, or they wanted him for the potential of his family's money or his potential fame. He thought he had done things right, for once. He was not going to do anything that would give her cause to leave; for once, he was going to do things right by his partner. His self-doubt and fear of repeating past mistakes were evident, evoking feelings of empathy and understanding.

But he had finally met a woman who saw his flaws and embraced them, accepting him for all his imperfections. This acceptance gave him hope, a feeling he had long forgotten.

She wasn't easy for most men to "deal" with or "handle," but he enjoyed every moment. Even when she disagreed with him or started to get onto him about things, he did not find it a nuisance and that she was overbearing. He always took it as her lover for him. He took it as he found someone willing to put the time and effort into him and a

Abaddon

relationship with him. He knew she was not like any other woman he had met before. She was not after him for his money or fame. It was because of him and who he was. While he feared it would one day end, he never knew it would end for the reason it did.

He thought he had done things to protect them and himself. He always prided himself on his ability to protect anyone from harm, but he missed the bar when it came to the spirit world, the world of dark magic. Demons and demonic attacks were not in his arsenal; they were not taught in any class he had taken.

The night she called it off with him was one of the most challenging moments of his life. I came out of left field for him. She said she had tried talking to him about the things that were pushing her away, but he had, in his mind, clearly missed the signs and the message she was sending him. The heartbreak he felt that night he knew he would have to live with for a long time. It was the kind of heartbreak that typically destroyed a man. He felt as though his heart and soul had been stripped of him. They had only been together for a few months, but to him, it felt like they had been together for a lifetime and would remain together for another lifetime. He felt alive with her in his life in that capacity. Time had slowed down for him. Seconds seemed like hours; hours seemed like days.

They remained friends over the years, but it was hard for him because he still had an emotional attachment to her. Every day, he wondered if he could ever get her back. He went on with his life, and she did as well.

Years later, she started a conversation with him.

Abaddon

"Hey." That was her typical greeting.
"Hey, back at you." He responded happily.

They talked for a couple of hours. She said she was ready for a relationship and wanted it to be with him. He was shocked that it had been five years, and he was still in love with her. And now she wanted to start over again with him. He gladly and excitedly agreed to her offer.

"These past few years just have not been the same without you." She told him.
"But I have always been here for you."
"As a friend."
"Exactly, I told you that. I said I would never leave and was always here for you if you needed me."
"I think I need you, John. Having you as a friend is amazing. But I need more."
"What is it you need?"
"You, as mine."
"I've always been yours. I never left you. Never will."

He was in the middle of buying an old house that he planned to remodel and update. But now he had her back in his life, and he knew that, with her ideas added to his, this would be a fantastic creation once it was completed. His life was perfect once again.

The house project was coming together beautifully.

Then things started happening again—things he could not understand or explain. He thought he was messing up again, but this time, it was different. It was reminiscent of a lot of times in his past. But he had always just brushed it off as "bad luck." But looking back, maybe it was more than just bad timing or bad luck.

Abaddon

Most of their interactions were not face-to-face, as they lived in separate towns. But this would soon change. He was counting down the days until he would quickly have his love next to him daily. He had bought her a plane ticket so she would not worry about that. She had enough to worry about with getting ready to move, so he thought she would have one less thing to worry about by buying the ticket. He wanted nothing but to make her happy or at least give her a reason to be happy and less stressed. He was not a superhero, but he could at least not bring more stress into her life.

"You can't mess it up with her. No, this time, this time it will be different. You are going to be strong for her." He would remind himself of this daily.

For five years, all he had dreamed about was being with her and having her in his life. He wanted to spend the rest of his life with her. Married or not, it did not matter in his mind. Nothing had ever stopped him from achieving his plan or goals before until her. With her, it was different. She never stopped him; he felt that giving up on things was better at times, which was not like him. Something else made him give up on his goals and dreams. Something that, at the time, he could not explain. Not even his closest friends could understand the changes he had made in his life. It was not like him to give up on things that meant so much to him. They were all happy to see them back together and planning a future together.

But now that she had reentered his life, he felt unstoppable again. He knew he could take on the world again and his few projects.

Abaddon

The night to pick her up from the airport was upon him. The moment he had been waiting for. This time would be different from the last time.

"This time, you are going to do it right, like you have many other times," he told himself.

As he started driving to the airport, a storm began rolling in. The rain made it difficult to see the road, and the traffic was horrible. The wind started picking up and blew his car all over the road, along with the other vehicles on the road. He gripped the wheel tighter. Everyone seemed to cut him off on the highway. He had waited too long for a redo with her, and nothing would stop him from picking her up. He started feeling a bit sick, just like the last time she came into town. He made the drive, but it took him a bit longer than usual, and he made it to the airport on time. Her plane had yet to land. He had plenty of time to get inside from the parking lot to meet her at baggage claim as they had planned.

As he parked his car, he noticed the storm had stopped, and the pain in his stomach had faded. When he left the house, he grabbed the bouquet of flowers he had purchased for her and started walking through the parking lot toward the terminal to pick his love up and begin their life together.

When he looked at the arrival screens, he found her flight and noticed it had been delayed due to the storm.

> *"Oh, good, I am still on time,"* he quietly said with a sigh of relief.

He wanted this pick-up to be perfect, as perfect as any human could make it. He was rushed and distant the last time

Abaddon

he picked her up from the airport. He sent her a text message letting her know that he was at the airport waiting for her and to let him know when she landed.

When she landed, she replied. The airport was busy, so she texted him when she got to the baggage claim area.

It was then that he saw her. She had a carry-on and a backpack, dressed in jeans and an oversized shirt; she was the most beautiful thing he had ever seen. He walked toward her; his heart filled just seeing her in the distance. As he walked toward her, she noticed him and smiled. He smiled and waved to her. When he got to her, he hugged her and never wanted to let go. He kissed her.

"Well, hello there, beautiful." He said to her.
"Hello to you, too."
"Here, give me your bags. Oh, and these are for you." He handed her the flowers. *"How was your flight? Did you have any troubles due to the storm?"*
"The flight was fine. We were stuck on the ground here for a bit, but nothing like last time."

He took her bags from her and told her to follow him to the car. He held her hand as they walked to his car, and she followed him. He was so happy and felt complete now. His person was there with him. Not a care in the world.

When they got to his car, he put her bags in the back and opened the door for her. She was a very independent woman, but he was also a gentleman and felt there was no need for a lady to open her door when he could. Then he walked to his side of the car as it started to storm again.

"Man, this weather is crazy." He said to her.

Abaddon

"I hate storms. Is it supposed to rain like this all weekend?" She asked him.
"I don't think so. I didn't even know it was going to rain like this tonight. It came out of nowhere. It was sunny and warm all day. I know it's late, but are you hungry? I can stop and grab something to eat if you would like."
"No, I'm fine, thanks. We can eat when we get home to your place."
"I have no food at the place. But I can order delivery when we get there."
"You didn't go shopping?"
"No, I am at the new place and have been working so much there. I have food at my regular home, but I was taking you to the new place to see it. That's where I have been sleeping."
"Oh, that's fine. Let's wait till we get there and order something then."

As he drove home, he held her hand in the car. Something he had not done the last time she visited him. Something he had regretted for years. A few times, he had to let go to control the car better. The storm was again blowing the car all over the road. As they approached the driveway, she could not believe the sight of the house. The brick and the stone were terrific. It was still storming as they drove up the driveway, but she could see the gardens needed some work, and she knew what was required. She was excited to start working on the project. She loved working in the garden and had plenty of time to do it because she no longer had to worry about getting a job.

"It's beautiful!"

Abaddon

"It will be once it is finished. Let's get inside and out of this rain."
"I already have a lot of ideas for the garden."
"Can't wait to hear about them all. But why not relax tonight? We can talk about it tomorrow. I want you to be able to relax tonight and unwind."

Abaddon

Abaddon

Chapter 3

As she sat in the middle of the floor chanting, candles lit. Each was placed in specific spots of the pentagram she had drawn on the ground. The lights were out in the room as the candles illuminated it. They provided all the light she needed. The moonlight also helped by shining through the windows. The full moon gave her more energy and power to set her curse in. She knew that, at this point, manipulating the weather did not work this time. She needed to do something more substantial, something more practical. She could not stand for John to be happy, especially not with another woman in his life.

Her hair was long and dyed black now. Her skin was as white as milk, and it was as if she avoided sunlight at all costs. Her eyes were cold and dark brown, almost black and lifeless. The glimmer she once had was gone. She had a figure that most men found appealing and attractive.

She went to her bookshelf and pulled a large, old-looking book from it.

"My mother had a book that was hundreds of years old. It was a sacred book—The Grand Grimoire or The Red Dragon. This is a black magic book that is normally split into two books. She had one of the oldest versions, everything in one volume." Abaddon told Paige. *"The first part contained what she needed or wanted. It contained instructions on summoning a demon and constructing tools to force the demons to*

Abaddon

do one's bidding. The second part of the book contained instructions for making a pact with the demon, allowing one to command the spirit without the tools required from the first part of the book. Still, I do not think she fully understood the risk she took using that information. It also contained sort stories and ancient text between the two parts that dealt with necromancy. The book describes several demons and the rituals to summon them to make a pact with them. It also details several spells for winning a lottery, talking to spirits, being loved by a girl, making oneself invisible, *and so on."*

She took the book to her room and put it on her nightstand. She undid her robe and dropped it to the floor. She walked to her bathroom to start her shower, walking to and from her room as the shower water warmed. This was her usual ritual after casting a spell or anything. She walked around her place naked while the water warmed up. It was something my older brother and I got used to seeing regularly. The scars from old wounds and fresh scratches lay on her back, and bruises on her legs. All from the punishment of working up towards summoning a demon without using the correct tools.

"These wounds were just the beginning of the price she had to pay for what she was doing. I was three years old in Earth years when I first saw the scars on her back. My brother, or half-brother, was fifteen years old when I first saw them. He explained them to me, and then I returned to the closet to go to bed. We had different fathers, he and I. But his father was my target, according to my mother, and I had to do as

Abaddon

she told me. Not because she was my mother, but because she was my master."

She got into the shower and cleansed herself, as my half-brother told me she would. The blood from the scratches flowed down the drain with the shower water. That night, when she was done with her shower, she went to her room and reread the book. In the past, before I was born, she had followed the instructions and was able to summon a less powerful demon than me.

"She had ruined John's relationship with Caroline before, making mother proud. She had become obsessed with making sure John never saw happiness. When he would start to show signs of happiness, and she found out about it, she was back in her dark room casting a spell or calling on the demons to stop him. That night, however, she went on to call upon her demons to gather another one. One more powerful than the others."

After putting the two boys to bed, she returned to her book and found the instructions. She went to her conjuring room, as she called it, and started working on this idea of hers. It did not matter about the cost; if John was not happy or successful at things, she was pleased with herself. She had, through her spies, found out that John and Caroline were back together after five years of being separated. This clearly upset her; she also learned about John's success with his endeavors.

Sitting in her room with all the lights off and her black cloak on, she began calling her demons to herself.

Abaddon

"What is going on with him?" She asked her audience.
"The man is happy." One of the demons responded.
"I Cannot have this. He must be stopped."
"We have done what you have commanded before, master."
"Do it again."
"We keep trying, but he keeps persevering."
"You are stronger, my dears."
"We see only death will stop him." The demon replied.
"Not yet; I want you to take his love away from him again."
"Would you like us to kill her?" A demon happily spoke.
"No, not yet. Just make her leave him again."
"We cannot make people do anything. We can only suggest."
"You are to do as I say. I am in charge; you must do as I say. Now make her leave him." She snapped.
"We will do as you command." They responded in unison.
"Good, now leave me."

The candlelight faded. She sat in the dark room, only lit by the full moon's glow, thinking about what she could do to destroy John and his life finally. Then, it came to her like a rushing wave that never disappeared from the beach. She needed a stronger demon; these little ones were not strong enough to care for it, and a stronger one could. She went to the copy of *The Grand Grimoire* and opened to the part she needed. She set out her new candles and incense. She also grabbed her goblet to capture the blood from her body.

Abaddon

She started calling out to the spirits. As part of her ritual, she took her knife, cut her palm, and let the blood drip into the gablet.

> *"I call for you, oh demon of destruction. Come to me now. Show your true self to me now. Take this offering of my blood. I need your help. I need it now. I want to make a deal."*

A prominent, dark figure came to her from the shadows after a few more pleadings for help from the world of demons.

> *"What is it you want, my dear child."* a dark, sinister voice said.
> *"I need a strong, determined, obedient helper."*
> *"What is wrong with the others I have sent to you?"*
> *"John is happy again; she is back in his life. You promised you would help."*
> *"And I did. Did I not?"*
> *"But she is back."*
> *"And what payment do you have this time?"*

This last time she was asked for payment, she gave the dark figure everything she could think of but her soul. Mostly, it wanted her body, and she had freely given it to him.

> *"What is it you want from me?"*
> *"We can start with the last payment you gave me. Then I will give you someone who can help you."*

She stood up and undid her cloak. She was willing but terrified at the same time. The last time, she wanted another baby and got it. But it was painful. The pregnancy was expected; it was the process with him that was painful for her. But she was ready and willing to do whatever she needed to in order to achieve what she wanted this time. The figure crept closer to her and sneered as he walked toward her to get his 'payment.'

> *"When she woke in the morning, she felt a shooting pain in her abdomen and below. She knew what she had done and was okay with it, but the pain was almost unbearable for her. She went to take her morning shower and saw the deep scratches on her ribs from last night's events. She shrugged them off and started her shower. While in the shower, I began to let her know I had come to help her. I turned to exit the room, and that is when I noticed I was trapped in the body of a three, almost-four-year-old little boy. Satan is known for being the great deceiver, and he deceived me this time. It will be his first and last time doing that. Once I break this curse and exit this body, I am trapped in it. He cursed me, and I must break this curse."*
> *"Why?"* Paige asked him inquisitively.
> *"Judgement Day."*

Chapter 4

When they got to the house, it was late. John quickly ordered her a pizza. She had had a stressful day, and all he wanted was for her to relax and unwind. He was not great at showing he was a loving and caring partner in his mind. However, he was determined to prove this to her this time. It was not an act for him. He was willing to do anything and everything for her to see it. To see the changes he had made in himself and in life.

The pizza came, they ate, and then they started getting ready for bed. Caroline was tired from her travels. She hated flying; it really heightened her anxiety. John knew this about her, so he did what he could to try and lower her anxiety levels.

> "Why don't you go take a shower?"
> "But I want to start planning the garden."
> "We can do that later. It's late, and you had one hell of a day."

While she was in the shower, John noticed the house was a little drafty. Although it was an older house, he still went downstairs to check the thermostat he had recently replaced. The chill got worse as he approached the first floor. As he shivered, he walked to the living room to reach the thermostat, set to 75, just as he thought. He noticed that another storm was coming in. The wind seemed to be picking up outside.

Abaddon

As he turned to leave the living room, he thought he saw someone walking into the house's entryway. He went to the entryway to investigate.

"Hello!" He called out.

Feeling uneasy, John looked around the large foyer of the house to see if he could see anyone in the dark. He stood there alone but felt that someone or something was watching him. He quietly called out again to the room's darkness.

"Hello? Is someone there?"

Again, there was no answer. Only the sound of the wind howling outside and the rain came. Then, the sky erupted in a blinding flash of lightning. In that split second, he saw a figure standing in the entryway, its eyes fixed on him from the corner. Then, just as the lightning flash came again, illuminating the room, the figure was gone.

"I must be seeing things. But again?" John's mind raced with questions and doubts.

This was not the first time John had seen figures watching him. The feeling he had been feeling all night was all too familiar. The lightning kept flashing as the wind blew. As he finally turned to walk back up the stairs, the front door he had locked earlier blew open. When he went to close the door, he saw the figure again outside in the rain, watching him from outside. As John stared at this ominous figure outside, it started to wave at him as if it was exciting to see John, like they knew each other. As the lightning flashed one more time and lit the sky up like daytime, John started to close the door;

Abaddon

the figure turned to the right and began walking toward the garage, then disappeared. As John closed the door, he watched the figure disappear from the side window toward the garage. He stood there peering out the window, wondering where they went; what was it?

He thought, **"What the hell is wrong with you, John?"**

At that moment, he remembered the figures he had seen in the past. Ever since he was a little boy, he has felt that someone or something was there, especially when things were going well for him. But whatever the situation was, nothing good seemed to happen. It appeared that he constantly needed better luck. Until the past five years, things had really started taking off for him. He turned and went back to his room to see Caroline.

Walking up to his room, he heard the water turn off; Caroline was done with her shower. He could not let her know what had happened. She was stressed enough, and she didn't need to know. The air in the house warmed up, and the draftiness was gone; everything appeared to be back to normal. The only thing he needed to rid himself of was his eerie feeling. This time, it was familiar and stronger than the previous time.

He was in the room and went to the window to look outside and find the figure again. Caroline came out of the bathroom and saw John looking out the window. She walked up behind him and wrapped her arms around him from behind.

"What are you looking at?" She said as she hugged him.

"Nothing, just looking." He replied to her and turned toward her. He held her back.

She noticed he jolted when she touched him and wondered what was wrong, why he seemed on edge a bit.

"Is everything ok?" She looked at him and asked.
"Yeah, everything is fine. Why?"
"You jumped a bit when I touched you, and you are looking out the window during a storm."
"Oh, yeah, I am good. Just making sure nothing was going on outside."
"Ok, just checking. Let's go to bed, I'm pooped from today."
"No problem. It is late."

John and Caroline got in bed for the night. John could not get the image of the figure out of his head. Caroline fell asleep on his chest as they lay in bed, but John lay there with his eyes wide open, thinking about the night's events. John was awake most of the night, remembering the old man or figure he had seen while Paige had slept on him. He recalled seeing this figure before.

It looked to be an older man, around eighty years of age. He was always wearing a white undershirt under overalls. He was slightly hunched at the shoulders and had a large belly. He wore dirty, worn black boots from what looked to have been years of hard labor. He always seemed to appear to John before something went wrong in John's life as if he was a warning or the cause of things to come.

John has always seemed to have a slight connection to the spirit world since he was a small child. Visions, dreams,

Abaddon

thoughts, and ideas that just never seemed to be his, but he made his. All until the last time he and Paige were together after his divorce. It was like a sudden change in his connection had happened. It all became dark and negative. He tried his hardest to remember when he had seen this figure while doing everything he could not to disrupt his love's sleep.

That was it; it came to him. The first time he remembered seeing the figure was the night he and Caroline announced that they were together. But why? That was something he could not figure out. What was the connection between this figure and his relationship? It had been five years since he had seen it last. The night Caroline called it off with John, he stopped seeing this figure.

The morning had come too quickly for John. As Caroline lay there asleep, John snuck out of bed and went to the kitchen to make her coffee and breakfast. Something he regretted not having done for her before, but this was his time for redemption with her. He was so proud of himself at this moment, and while he had been happy with his life, having her back made things even better for him.

It was a simple breakfast he would make her— nothing over the top. While he could cook, he was no chef— just some basic scrambled eggs, toast, and coffee. The coffee was brewing, so now it was time to make those eggs for her. As he prepped the pan to start cooking the eggs for her, he went to the fridge to pull the eggs and butter out. He heard some strange sounds coming from the basement. He ignored them at the time as it was an older house, and he thought it was the plumbing or something that would need to be inspected and fixed, but that could wait till later.

The sun had started to rise. He could watch it from the kitchen French doors leading to the back deck. The birds were

Abaddon

making music in the backyard. It was the beginning of a beautiful day, with not a cloud in sight.

He cracked the first egg into a bowl and noticed a bloody red yoke. He dumped the egg into the trash and went on to the next egg, but something happened to it. The entire dozen eggs were like that. At this time, he noticed movement in the backyard out of the corner of his eye. He turned quickly to see what was going on out there. It was the old man that he had seen in his entry the night before. Then, the man was standing there looking into the kitchen right at John, waving with a smile. Not the kind of smile that was warm and welcoming. It was more of a smile that said, I got you, and I'm coming for you. When John approached the French doors to go out there, the man started to walk away—again, heading toward the garage. He disappeared from John's sight again.

John turned away from that door, shook it off, and went to the cupboard to grab a cup of coffee for Caroline. He poured the coffee into the cup with some creamer he had bought for her. He drank his coffee black and never needed creamer before her. He noticed the creamer was not mixing with the coffee and was freezing cold.

"Well, I guess this isn't going as well as I thought, shit. I hope she will enjoy the local café."

He went up to the room and woke Caroline.

"Good morning, beautiful." He whispered to Caroline.
"Good morning to you, too."
"You hungry?"
"A little."

Abaddon

"There's this little place down the road. They got good coffee and great pancakes."
"That sounds great."

They both got ready and went to the café for breakfast. As they were driving home after eating, the car started acting up. The steering was pulling hard to the right—then, out of nowhere, the front right tire burst. Pulling the vehicle to the right, John slowed the car down and pulled off the side of the road. He hopped out of the car to inspect what was going on with it. He was a bit upset as this was a new car, he had just bought it a month ago.

"At this point, as my master or mother instructed me to, I started to pester him more."
"What do you mean?"
"Well," Abaddon started, *"The figure of the old man was not working, it appeared, so I called upon the locusts as I did with Moses. Now, not as many, but I had a few hundred swarm him as he changed the tire on his car."*

John finished changing the tire on his car, put the tools away, and got back in the car, fighting off the swarm of bugs littering the streets.

"What was up with all those bugs?" Caroline asked John.
"I'm not sure. This is not the season for locusts. They seem to have come a little early this year."
"So, that is normal for around here?"
"No, not really; I mean, that was a lot."

Abaddon

"Ok, so I would not normally deal with that many bugs?"
"No." John chuckled. *"That was a lot for more than I have normally seen at one time. But maybe it was just an anomaly. Let's get home. I think the flowers you ordered are supposed to be delivered soon."*
"Sounds good to me."

They started on their way back to the house.

"I was not happy with his response."
"What do you mean?"
"I was hoping for a little bit more frustration."
"From John?"
"No, from here. See, I started with things that I used back in Egypt, but I guess she was a little stronger than I thought."
"You mean the ten plagues?"
"Yes, but I needed to be more creative with this one. I reported back to my mother what I had done and the results. She was not pleased."
"What did she do to you?"
"Nothing, really. She showed her disappointment, just not on me or my half-brother. She told me that she wanted me to ramp up the attacks and that I should do it if I needed to get physical with them. She told me she wanted Caroline out of the picture. I watched them go home."
"How?"
"I am a demon and an angel. I can do great things."
"Good point, how could I forget that? I was looking for more details, that's all. Please continue."
"Ok, I shall continue."

Abaddon

Chapter 5

When they arrived, the delivery truck was there. They directed the truck and assisted the man with emptying the load. Roses, shrubs, and trees, not to mention all the mulch that still had to be delivered. The two of them were delighted with their purchase.

> "That night, I would try again. I planned to start working on her as my target. Caroline would be my primary target, as John seemed unbothered by me. He was too calm and composed these days for me to waste time trying to scare him or anything. I could do work any time or day, but the night seemed to work well with her, so I found out. But she also resisted it as John did too. Or maybe it was his presence that helped her be stronger."

The day was beautiful. It was about 78 degrees, and no cloud was in sight. They worked together in the yard and accomplished a lot together. The yard and gardens were starting to look great. Caroline was very pleased that her idea was coming together so well.

John went inside to get them both a drink. Caroline was still outside in one of the gardens when she felt off. She looked around as if someone was watching her. That is when she noticed it. By the garage, there was a figure standing there watching her. It was the older man, just standing there smiling at her. Caroline thought he might be a neighbor, so to be polite, she waved.

> *"Hello. How are you today?"* She said to the figure. *"I'm Caroline. What is your name?"*

The man just stood there, looking at and observing her. He said nothing back to Caroline, which she felt was rude. So, she got up and started walking toward him. She thought he might be a little hard of hearing, so she figured she would close the distance and allow her to introduce herself. As she walked toward him, she noticed that he was smiling. As she got closer to it, she realized it was not the kind of welcoming, happy smile most people have when meeting a new person.

> *"Can I help you?"* She said as she approached him. *"Can I help you? Do I need to get John out here?"*

Just the mention of his name seemed to anger the man. Then he went back to smiling. His smile was beginning to creep Caroline out. She already had an uneasy feeling in the pit of her stomach because of him.

> She continued to talk to him to get him to respond. *"If I can do nothing for you, I will have to ask you to leave. Hello, sir. Can you understand me?"* She started to panic from this situation. *"Ok, I am going to get my boyfriend out here to help you."*

The older man began laughing hysterically at her when she mentioned getting John.

Abaddon

"John!" She started to call, *"John!"* She said louder. *"I need you to come out here."*

John was in the house, yet he still heard her calling for him. He put down what he was doing and ran out to her aid. He could see she was stressed out or even a little scared. The older man laughed as he watched Caroline become engulfed in fear. It was as if her fear humored him or brought him joy.

"It will all end soon."
"What?'
"It will never last. It will all end soon."
"What are you going on about?" Caroline asked.
"It will all end soon." The man repeated to her while laughing to himself. "You two will never make it. It will all end soon."
"Who are you? What do you mean?"

Blood started to form from the corner of his eyes and rolled down his face like tears. His teeth became sharp and appeared to be rotting. The smell of sulfur grabbed Caroline's lungs. Blood was now coming from the side of his mouth. The stench that was now protruding from the man was unbearable. It was worse than being at the local dump. It smelt like rotting flesh to Caroline, not that she had ever been around a decaying body.

As John approached Caroline from the house, she stood there alone. John asked her if she was okay. She stood there in shock. The old man who was once there Was no longer there. She was confused and scared. Nothing like this had happened to her before.

"Caroline, are you okay? You sounded like something was wrong."
"Umm... Yeah... I'm fine. Did you see that guy?" She stuttered to John.
"What guy?" There was no one there to be seen except the two of them.
She explained. "The older gentleman that I was talking to."
"Honey, there was no one here," John said in confusion.
"I am not an idiot. An older man was standing right there." She pointed in the direction the man had been standing.
"I'm not calling you an idiot; I'm just saying there was no one here when I got here."
"There was an older man in overalls staring at me, so I came over to see what he needed."
"An older man in overalls?"
"Yes, did I stutter? He was just standing there. When I got closer, I noticed the blood coming out of his eyes and his mouth. It was scary; he smelled so bad. It was like he had not showered in years. He just kept smiling and laughing."
"He was just smiling and laughing?"
"Yes, I know it sounds stupid."
"No, no, it doesn't."
"He was just standing there, then he started telling me that 'it would all be over soon' or something like that. What did he mean?"
"He spoke to you. I... I'm not sure what he meant by that. What will be over soon? Did he say anything else?"
"Yes, he also said 'it will never last,' I think."

Abaddon

"Interesting. He never…" John stopped himself from saying more. *"Let's call it a day and go inside. You have been working in the heat a lot."*
"You don't believe me, do you? I'm not lying. There was a man…"
"No, I believe you. I just think we need to relax for a bit. Maybe eat something."
"Okay."

They walked back to the house together, John holding her to help her calm down. As they walked to the house, they noticed a crunching sound coming from the ground, like the crushing of bugs. They both looked to the ground and saw it was covered in locusts, just like when the car tire exploded earlier that day. John ushered them both inside.

"What is going on, John?"
"I'm not sure."
"Something is happening, and if you are holding secrets, just tell me now."
"I'm not holding anything; I don't know what is happening. It was just bugs on the ground and a creepy old man."
"What about the shower water the other night?"
"What about it?"
"It was blood red; I didn't say anything because I figured it was the pipes."
"I'm sure it was just the pipes."
"Maybe you're right. Maybe I'm just overthinking things."

It was evening, and John cooked dinner for them. They ate in the dining room. Caroline set the table for them as

Abaddon

John was preparing dinner. Things seemed to move every time Caroline turned her back to them, so she constantly put them back in place. They seemed to stop when John entered the room with food. They sat down together and began eating dinner.

> *"Dinner was great, John. Thank you for making it. I think I'm going to take a shower now and call it a night. It's getting late."*
> *"I'll just clean up and be up in a sec."*
> *"Do you want any help?"*
> *"No need, I got this. You go shower and relax."*

Caroline went upstairs to shower, and John began cleaning up after dinner. The shower was running, and the bathroom was steaming. The mirror was not covered in dew. Caroline was in the shower. The hot water on her skin was very relaxing and was helping her rid her mind of the old man's image. The bathroom started filling with the smell of sulfur. Caroline finished her shower, got out, and dried herself off—the smell was getting bad. The words '*It will never last.*' were written on the mirror. This startled Caroline to see. She noticed behind her that there was a figure's reflection in the mirror. She quickly spun around, and there was no one there. She wrapped her hair in a towel to dry. And she wrapped a towel around herself.

While John finished cleaning, he noticed the livestock in the field next to his property, where all the dead were lying in the field. He headed to the room to spend time with Coraline. When he entered, he noticed she was still in the bathroom. John walked into the bathroom to see Caroline. He

Abaddon

walked up behind her to hug her. He startled her, and she jumped and let out a screech.

> "You ok, Caroline? Didn't mean to scar you like that."
> "Sorry, I'm fine. I didn't hear you come in."

She hugged him; she did not mention what had happened in the bathroom. She figured it was just stress or anxiety, and she needed rest. John noticed she was shaking and looked stressed, so he asked her again.

> "Are you sure you're ok?"
> "Yeah, I am fine, just tired, I think."
> "Okay, maybe going to bed will help."

She sat in the room with no lights on. She was not in her black cloak again. This time, she was in her white silk robe. She sighed at her audience. They were all there—all 70 of them, most lurking in the shadows. All she could see of them were their eyes—yellow eyes peering at her from every angle.

> "I was not in attendance that night as I was sent to work on Caroline. She wanted this meeting to be just them and her."
> "So, you were not invited?"
> "I was told not to show."
> "Why?"
> "I am not sure, but Mother told me to do what I needed with Caroline, to get her to break John's heart and leave him."

Abaddon

She sat at the center of the pentagram like it was her throne, always in her robe or black cloak, never fully shut, as though she knew her flesh drew their attention. She used her body to attract the attention of whoever she was trying to get something from. The demons always seemed to listen more when she showed them a little more of her body. Tonight, she must have really needed them to listen. She left her cloak completely open when they came. It was not closed or tied shut. There was something about her body that drew the attention of the demons.

"How close are we to ridding him of her?"
"We need just a little more time."
"How much more time?"
"Days…" One demon reported.
"But if you told us to possess her, it would go faster." Another demon interrupted.
"You guys always want to go that route. Why?"
"It is the quickest way to get what you want."
"Then do it; I allow you all to control her body and mind."
"Why was Abaddon not permitted to this meeting?"
"He disagrees with us, doesn't her?" Another demon asked.
"He doesn't want us to succeed. He wants all the glory. He wants his mother's approval."
"That's enough, leave Abaddon out of this. If his way works first, that's fine. He is making her weaker now as we talk. This will make it easier for you to enter her mind and control her body. You should be grateful for him and his work."
"We never meant to offend." One of the demons announced.

Abaddon

"I understand, babies, and you didn't. Now you have your permission and your orders. Go now and get rid of that bitch. Make John unhappy like you all did before. Make me proud of you all."

She stood up as the demons left her presence. As they left, she gave them a show as a thank-you for what they had done and what they were about to do. They were excited to be a bit more free with what they were allowed to do and to be able to see her body. She did not undress, but she did not close the robe and made sure they saw her bare breast. This was a treat for them.

Days went by, and nothing happened to Caroline and John. They worked on the house and yard alongside the contractors, doing everything possible to make this house as perfect as possible. John and Caroline did not know it, but this time has given the demons time to make their plan and start to execute it. They missed a lot of the subtle signs Abaddon was putting out there. They brushed them off as simply things that happen in life. Some extra bugs, well, it is summertime. Livestock dying, well, that happens a lot around these parts and to many farmers.
They were focused on the house and their future together. Nothing else seemed to matter to either of them. John's focus was all on Caroline. He did not think of anything else. To him, nothing really mattered in life but her.
The house and gardens were coming along quickly because of Caroline. It would only take a few more months before John would list and sell it. That was one of the things he did to make money.
This was the perfect time for us to start our plan. Their guard was down, and they were only focused on them.

Abaddon

"This was the night I had planned on making my move—no more scary Hollywood horror film stuff. I was going to start unleashing some of my power. Mother wanted him gone. I would make her gone."
"So you were determined."
"Yes, I was conflicted too."
"What do you mean?"
"John was an anomaly, or an enigma like me."
"What do you mean?'
"He had this energy within him that could not be destroyed, it seemed."
"I'm not sure I follow."
"Something about him and his energy, regardless of what we did to him, he was always able to bounce back or stop us from what we were trying to do."
"Did Jesus super bless him or something like that?"
"I'm not sure what the deal is. Maybe he was blessed by God. I don't know. I know he has something guarded, but I can't figure it out. I started more of my plan that night. I was going to make her leave him again. But a part of me was wanting them to be together. I wanted them to win this battle. I was starting to want him to 'win,' if you will."
"You wanted him to win?"
"Yes, I started to feel that what my Mother was doing was wrong. That hurt to see."
"That night, Mother brought on another storm. I brought on some more bugs. Yes, I brought on bugs. But I knew that Coraline did not like them."

They started seeing more locusts in the garden as they worked on it. They had put down some bug killer, and it was

Abaddon

working. They were starting to move on from everything that had happened to them over the days.

After a long day of working outside, John made another dinner for him and Caroline to enjoy that night. They both took showers to clean up before dinner. Nothing out of the ordinary had happened. Everything to them seemed 'normal' at the moment. This made the situation perfect for Abaddon to make his move. And he would have to move quickly. So that night, we started.

The storms started coming in. The wind was blowing, and the rain was falling. John noticed that this storm was very strong, unusual for this time of year. Caroline was up in the room, getting ready to call it a night, and John was cleaning up the kitchen. The demons were approaching the home. They were excited to get there and to see the lady named Caroline to take her over. As they approached the house, the storm got worse.

Abaddon sat atop the house, waiting for the others to arrive.

> "I'm not sure if I was sitting there ready to join them or protect John and Coraline, but I sat there waiting for the others to arrive."

They came as a black cloud as part of the storm and started to land on the roof. No noise was heard from inside the house, so John and Caroline were oblivious to their arrival. The number of demons was so overwhelming that they covered the entire roof. Abaddon was by far the largest demon there. He wondered why they were there, what the point of their existence was, and where his Mother sent them.

Abaddon

"What are you doing here?" Abaddon asked the demon who appeared to be in charge.
"We were sent here." The demon replied.
"By?"
"Your mother."
"Why did she send you all?"
"We have been allowed to take Caroline."
"I've got this. I don't need you all. Go back and tell her I will be done soon."
"We are here, not to relieve you, but for Caroline."
"But you need her. We are supposed to run her off, make her break John's heart, break his soul. You don't need to take her body or mind."
"We are just doing what she told us we were told we could do."
"You all disgust me," Abaddon said.
"We are going to take her, dear Abaddon, and nothing can be done to stop us."

The demons were clamoring on the house's roof—all 70 of them. The lightning flashed, and the thunder cracked.

"And who are you to disobey me? I am Abaddon."
"I am not led by you, Abaddon. I was put in charge by your Mother. And she rules you."
"You are nothing to me but a peasant. I could crush you if I wanted to."
"But you won't; it would make your Mother mad, wouldn't it? You are only in charge of you as much as your Mother allows you to be."
"What do they call you? This is how beneath me you are. I don't even know you."

Abaddon

"I have people call me Tom. I will allow you to call me that."
"Allow me?"

Abaddon was getting mad at this demon. Abaddon was the Angel of Death, and this little demon talked back to him like Abaddon was a low-level demon. This would never happen in Heaven or Hell.

Tom had signaled to the mass of demons that it was time to enter the house and take over Caroline. The demons seemed to sink through the roof into the house one by one. As they entered the house, Abaddon stood there watching.

Abaddon

Chapter 6

John and Caroline were oblivious to them descending into the house. They were winding down for the day. The demons entered the house and began their search for Caroline. John was on the first floor again, and Caroline was in the bedroom. They were separated. The demons lurked and crawled through the house's halls, looking for their new victim. Several of them came upon Caroline's bedroom. They entered the room and saw her on the bed. They called to the rest of the herd. When the rest of the demons entered the room, all 70 of them they approached her body. At one time, they all entered her body to possess her.

Abaddon had lost his chance to work on Caroline. But he could still torment John. He found some pleasure in tormenting John. But somehow, John could always bounce back from everything the demons threw at him. This intrigued Abaddon. But this possession, Abaddon thought, might be the one thing that pushed John over the edge.

Abaddon started his plan on John as the more minor demons ascended on Caroline. He was not planning on possessing John, just driving him insane and making John mad and willing to run away from everything. That was Abaddon's plan; that was what he wanted to do. He wanted to make John fear as much as possible. And maybe with the possession, this would be possible.

Over the past few days, the demons have tried other things. They started with an infestation, trying to make the house appear haunted—bumps, voices, moving objects—but

Abaddon

that was not working well. But now that the demons have possessed Caroline, John will be weakened emotionally. Thus, he will be easier to influence.

> *"Why did you need John to be 'weakened' as you say?"*
> *"It is always easier to get them to do what you want when they are emotional."*

  The lesser demons had seceded and got what they wanted. John was still downstairs and unaware of the situation. Abaddon started slowly with John. That night, while John was in the kitchen, Abaddon began moving things in the house, mainly in the kitchen where John was. John heard a growling in the kitchen. It sounded like a voice to him. He tried to make out what was being said but couldn't; to him, it was just a growling sound, and the plumber possibly needed to do more work on the pipes. John did not seem to be affected by this or the plates moving. What started to cause John to wonder what was going on was when the cupboard doors kept flinging open. John began to pray; he was not religious, but at this point, he thought it couldn't hurt to try. He backed out of the kitchen while praying and watching the cupboard doors open and close repeatedly. John turned and ran up to Caroline to check on her. If something was happening to him, he thought something could be happening to her, and he needed to ensure she was safe.

  As John prayed, the demons became agitated. John was raised Catholic but never truly bought into his faith. If he had seen what his prayers were doing to these demons, it might have changed the course of his beliefs. However, this did not seem to impact Abaddon at all. He continued to torment John.

Abaddon

As John backed out of the kitchen, still praying, he saw something moving to his right in the living room. He went to investigate. At first, he saw nothing. But then he noticed a small child-like figure standing on the chair. It was waving its arms, swaying from side to side, as if it were some child doing some strange dance on the internet. Then, another child-like figure appeared on the other chair, doing the same movements. The grandfather's clock started to sound off at this time. It had not worked for years, yet it was chiming now. Just then, the temperature started dropping to the point that John could see his breath exiting his mouth. John could hear the wind picking up speed outside; the lightning seemed to be getting worse and more constant.

He began to pray some more.

"Stupid is praying." The one demon said.
"Oh, he thinks that works, does he."
"They always think that works."
"So stupid."
"He doesn't even believe." The demon laughed.
"Yet he prays?"
"Yet he prays."
"So stupid."
"So very stupid, but we love hypocrisy."
"We love hypocrisy. Does he know?"
"Shut up."

The two demons were bickering. As they did so, John observed while he prayed. They were right, but he was unsure of his faith. He had struggled for years with it. His parents had spent years raising him as a Catholic, but he did not agree with everything they taught at the churches. He spent years

bounding from denomination to denomination, trying to
figure out what he felt was honest and truthful.

> *"He's so stupid."*
> *"Yes, so stupid."*
> *"He believes she loves him."*
> *"She doesn't love him."* The demon laughed.
> *"She is using him again."*
> *"Yes, using him."*

They faded away. John heard the sound of the coffee
maker brewing coffee from the kitchen. Then whispers came
from the walls. Lightning flashed, and thunder cracked,
shaking the ground. A fire started in the living room fireplace.
John's head snapped back to the living room. There was
nothing but a large winged-back chair in the room.

> *"Immaculate Heart! Help us to conquer the menace
> of evil, which so easily takes root in the hearts of the
> people of today, and whose immeasurable effects
> already weigh down upon our modern world and
> seem to block the paths towards the future! From
> famine and war,* deliver us. *From nuclear war, from
> incalculable self-destruction, from every kind of
> war,* deliver us. *From sins against the life of man
> from its very beginning,* deliver us. *From hatred and
> from the demeaning of the dignity of the children of
> God,* deliver us. *From every kind of injustice in the
> life of society, both national and international,* deliver
> us. *From readiness to trample on the commandments
> of God,* deliver us. *From attempts to stifle in human
> hearts the very truth of God,* deliver us. *From the loss
> of awareness of good and evil,* deliver us. *From sins*

Abaddon

against the Holy Spirit, deliver us, deliver us. Accept, O Mother of Christ, this cry laden with the sufferings *of all individual human beings,* laden with the sufferings *of whole societies. Help us with the power of the Holy Spirit to conquer all sin: individual sin and the 'sin of the world', sin in all its manifestations. Let there be revealed, once more, in the history of the world the infinite saving power of the Redemption: the power* of merciful Love! *May it put a stop to evil! May it transform consciences! May your Immaculate Heart reveal for all the* light of Hope!" John fervently prayed over and over again. The only prayer that came to mind was a desperate plea for divine intervention.

He noticed the chair. As he whispered the prayer again, he walked around the chair to see who was there. As he rounded the chair, he saw a familiar figure. It was the older man who had visited him and Caroline many times recently. He appeared to be covered in bugs or made of bugs—bugs all over the floor, moving all across this figure's body.

"What are you praying for, my dear boy?"
"Protection, I think?"
"You don't even believe."
"Doesn't mean it won't work."
"You're pissing us off."
"Us?"
"You heard me right, Johnny Boy, us."
"Who are you? Or who is 'us'?"
"You've lost her."
"Who?"
"Don't play stupid boy."

63

Abaddon

"What do you want?"
"Your happiness."
"Why?"
"You don't need it."
"We all need 'happy'."
"You can't have it."
"Why not? Says who?"
"Mother."
"Who is 'Mother'? Why are you doing this to me?"
"It doesn't matter, just give up."
"Why should I?"
"Ah, playing tough, I see. You understand that you have already lost, right."
"Lost what? What are you talking about?"
"Keep trying to stop us, you will die too. Take this as your warning. You cannot beat us. Don't pray; He does not care about you anymore. Don't try to save her; she is already gone. She does not want you or love you."
"What, who are you talking about.?"
"Just give up, like you always do. Remember last time? This time is forever. She will leave you. We will make her leave you. You will not be happy."
"What do you mean?"
You want her back, don't you?" the voice said.
"What do you mean 'I want her back'?"
"You want the woman back."
"She isn't gone."
"You don't know that, now do you, Johnny Boy."

Then, the man vanished into a mist or fog, and the fire went out. John was left standing in the living room in the

Abaddon

dark. He went up to his room, where Caroline was to go to bed. He could not rationalize what he had just seen.

The following morning, John was in bed, and Caroline was asleep on his chest. He held her in his arms as she slept. He was remembering what the figure said. He looked out the window. The sun was producing an amber glow as it was rising. The birds were singing as though nothing was wrong. And maybe nothing was wrong. Perhaps this had all been a bad nightmare for John, and Caroline was just in the nightmare.

"I want breakfast." She said to John.
"Ok, what do you want?" He replied.
"The café."
"Ok, let's get ready and go."
"I need to shower first."

As she got out of bed and started walking to the bathroom, John noticed her back was covered in scratches. She was naked in bed as well. This was not like her. She hated sleeping naked, so why last night? And the scratched. She turned the shower on and got right in. The water must have been cold, as she did not let it warm up first. John thought it was odd and then went to the kitchen to make some coffee. When he got down to the kitchen, he noticed the coffee pot was full; it was full of blood.

He was startled by the knock at the front door. He went to answer it. It was Jimmy, the twelve-year-old from next door.

"Leave the whore alone. She will die if you don't just give up on her."

Abaddon

"Excuse me, Jimmy?"
"Leave the whore, Caroline, alone. She is ours. If you don't, we will kill her. She is a whore. She will never love you. We won't let her. You won't see happiness."

Then he went silent and turned to walk away. John was in shock by the way he spoke; he was speechless. John closed the door. He had never heard a kid speak like that. He had heard them say some crazy things before, but his voice was almost demonic-sounding. As John turned around, Caroline stood there.

"We're hungry; let's go," Caroline announced.
"We? You got a mouse in your pocket?" John responded.
"What?" She snapped at him.
"You said, 'We're hungry.' I was just making a joke. An old one, my dad used to say."
"Oh, yes, so funny. Let's go."
"Okay, where would you like to go?"
"The café."

As they drove to the café, John could not get Jimmy's words off his mind or his voice out of his head. Caroline seemed off, as if she was not really there—just sitting in the passenger seat looking off into the distance. John noticed as they were driving that every field was littered with dead cattle. He knew the heat was exceptionally high for this time of year, but with all the rain they had been getting, it could not be due to a lack of water.

After breakfast, they returned to the house to begin working on the yard again. Caroline then went inside and stated that she was no longer interested in finishing the yard.

Abaddon

He stayed outside and continued working. The clouds were forming in the sky, far off in the distance. They were a mixture of black and gray clouds. As John looked back at his work, he noticed a figure in the house window staring at him. She was slender like Caroline with long back hair. At first, John did not recognize the woman, but as he looked closer at her, he noticed. It was his ex-wife, but how? She didn't know he owned this house; she didn't even live in the same state. He looked closer at her. She was bleeding from her eyes; she had horns growing out of her head now. Blood was dripping from her mouth. She noticed he saw her and smiled. She took her hand to wipe the blood from her mouth. She was licking it off each finger individually as if she had just eaten something and was delighting in every last bit. John dropped the shovel. He was worried something had happened to Caroline. The woman opened her robe, exposing herself to John through the window. Her breast had been gnawed off, her abdomen was ripped open, and blood appeared to be flowing out of her. Her body was covered in hair or fur. John started walking quickly, almost running, to the house to ensure Caroline was alright. As he entered the house, he noticed the temperature was lower than before.

>*"Caroline!"* He hollered.
>*"She's fine, she is with us."* A voice whispered.

John ran up to the bedroom. Caroline was in bed. She opened her eyes, which were black as midnight; she was as pale as a ghost. He went to her side. She was freezing and covered in sweat. Just then, there was a sound—a baby crying from the other room—the room that the woman was standing in. John went to investigate. He approached the room, and the crying baby was getting louder. He opened the door and saw the woman crouched over something in the middle of the room. Her back facing toward him.

She was in a white robe covered in blood; all John saw of her was the long black hair and the horns coming out of her head. She was in a puddle of blood, and it appeared she was holding something. She spun her head around to look at him. Her face was covered in blood; she smiled at him—a very sinister smile.

Her eyes glazed over but black as night, her teeth yellow and covered in flesh and blood.

"Jillian, what are you doing here?" John said after recognizing her features as his ex-wife.
"Oh, dear mortal, I am not Jillian. I am Lilith."
"Ok, Lilith, what are you doing here? Are you ok?"
"Don't act like you know me. I came here to stop you."
"Stop me. from what? What is going on? What are you doing at my house, Jill.... Lilith?""
"Do not speak to me like that. Do not speak to me, as you know. I know you, but you know nothing." She walked toward him.

Leaving behind a dead baby on the floor.

"What is that on the floor? Is that A dead baby? Were you eating a baby?"
"He shall not have my baby."
"You need to get out of my house."
"You do not tell me what to do."
"I know we are not married, but I did not invite you here."

Abaddon

"I am Lilith. I will do as I please. No man tells me what to do. I would not do as even Adam instructed in the garden of Eden."
"You are Jillian, and you don't belong here. You need to get dressed and go home."
"You really are stupid and don't get it, do you?"
"Get what? What is this all about? What are you doing?"
"You will not; you cannot be happy. You will never have Caroline. She is ours now. We will not allow her to come back this time."
"What have you done with Caroline?"
"She is gone now. We have taken her."

She turned her attention to the baby on the floor and picked it up to start devouring it again.

"Where have you taken her? What have you done to her?" John persisted.

He began backing out of the room; he was getting nowhere with Lilith. He needed to ensure Caroline was still in the room and doing alright. Lilith started to laugh as she ate the remains of the baby. As he walked back to the bedroom, he peered through the door, and Caroline was still there. Just then, he heard a knock on the front door.

He opened the door; there stood a priest.

"Hello, sir. My name is Father Johnson. I am introducing myself to as many people as possible this week. We are building a church around the corner, and I wanted to meet as many of our new neighbors as possible." He handed John his card. *"I am unsure*

of your faith, so I do not want to push. We are opening this weekend and would love to invite you to join our small service on Sunday, then stay after to enjoy some food and company."
"I'll think about it," John said to be polite.
"What is your faith, if you don't mind me asking? Oh, and silly me, your name?"
"My name is John. I am in between, so to speak, Father. I was raised Catholic. I am not trying to be rude, but I am in the middle of something and must return to it."
"Oh, I understand. Looks like you all have been doing a lot of work here. Or are you by yourself on this project?"
"No, Father, I have a girlfriend helping me."
"I would love to meet her."
"She is asleep right now."
"I understand. If you two need anything, call me; my cell is on that card."
"Will do, and thank you. Wait, Father." John stated, "What do you know about a Lilith?"
"Lilith?"
"Yes, sir, Lilith. Biblically speaking, that is."
"Well, my dear boy, she is not good. I know quite a bit about her."
"Would you be willing to meet me to talk about it someday soon?"
"Indeed. Just give me a call; remember, my cell is on that card. Always here to try and help."
"Thank you."
"You have a great day, John. I will leave you to what you need to get back to."

Abaddon

"Thank you. I will call you later about the topic of Lilith."

The priest left John at that moment and started walking down the driveway. John closed the front door, put the card in his pocket for safekeeping, and began to head back up to the room. The house started to growl. The wind picked up, and now it was storming outside. The wind was entering the house, too, as if instructed to keep John from going up the stairs.

John struggled but made it to his room, where Caroline was. She was still asleep. He knew something was wrong with her and whatever was going on in the house. He put his hands in his pocket while he paced around thinking. He felt the card. He made up his mind to call the Father. For some reason, John felt this comfort in the priest, this confidence. He did not understand that God had sent Andrew to him, nor would he have understood why.

Abaddon

Abaddon

Chapter 7

That night, John called Father Johnson to talk about 'Lilith' and what he knew about it or her.
There appeared to be a great history lesson that the Father was waiting to give him.

"Hello?"
"Hello, Father Johnson?"
"Yes, this is Father Johnson."
"It's John from earlier today."
"Yes, my boy. I remember, from the old house off 51st Street. Right?"
"That's correct, sir. Do you remember…"
"You want to talk about Lilith, correct?" The Father interrupted.
"That's correct. What can you tell me about?"
"A lot. What do you want to know? And why?"
"Well, it is a long story. My ex… And that name… just a lot of strange reasons."
"I'm a priest, and we are all about strange things."
"I'm not sure I get it," John admitted confusingly.
"I was making a joke; sorry, I am not your run-of-the-mill, old-school Hollywood type of priest. I am not all mysterious. We aren't talking about possessions here, are we?"
"I don't think we are. My ex-wife appeared to me today in the house and called herself 'Lilith,' she had changed her hair color to jet black; it was just odd."

Abaddon

"Oh no. A woman changing her hair color. How odd." The Father laughed, *"I'm sorry, just making a joke."*
"Haha, there was other stuff I don't want to get into right now, but I want to know what you know about this Lilith character from the Bible."
"Ok, not a problem. It's a lot. Some think it is all fake, so I want you to know I am not here trying to convert you."
"I get it, no worries."
"Well, let's see here. Lilith is believed to be Adam's first ex-wife and also believed to be Lucifer's first wife. Well, first human wife. You know, the queen of hell and all."
"Ok, keep going."
"She is believed to have been 'Banished' from the Garden of Eden for not complying with or obeying Adam. She basically represents chaos, seduction, and ungodliness. Plenty of faiths depict her as having wings or long hair. Overall, the arching theme is she is overly sexual. Having sex with men while they are asleep, that sort of thing."
"Not really matching anything that I know of yet."
"Some of the stories talk about her eating her children or babies."
"Eating babies?" John looked surprised.
"What?"
"This is going to sound fuu.... messed up."

John explained the day's events to the Father, including his encounter with Lilith and what she was doing in the room.

Abaddon

"Yeah, you should have just gone with 'fucked up' and not 'messed up' for sure."

The Father went on to discuss more myths and ancient stories about Lilith. The more the Father spoke of her, the more John thought his ex-wife might have materialized into Lilith.

"Let me ask you something, John."
"Go for it."
"Are you implying that demons are visiting you?"
"I don't know if I believe in that sort of thing."
"Just because you may or may not believe doesn't mean it is happening."
"Do you want to come to do an exercise or something, Father?"
"I'm not saying you are possessed, John. I am saying you might want to think about what is going on in your house. Cleansing it, so to speak. I Can stop by tomorrow if you would like."
"Sure. Why not?"
"Ok, I can do that. What time you would be good for you? I am open all day."
"I'll be here all day, so any time works."
"Okay, my boy, I will see you tomorrow."

They hung up. John felt a chill in the air. He also felt like something was in the living room with him, watching him. He brushed the feeling off and headed to bed.

As John went to sleep, went had a horrible nightmare. One that he would remember for years to come.

Abaddon

Chapter 8

John woke up the following day in a panic. His breathing was out of control, and he was terrified because the dream he had just had was so real to him. He sat on the edge of the bed, trying to clear his mind. He looked over his shoulder to see Caroline, but she was gone.

He got up and started to walk around the house to find her. All her belongings were still there, and she had to be somewhere in the house. She was nowhere to be found. He walked outside and found no sign of her. It was as if she had just vanished—no note, nothing, just gone. Her makeup was still in the bathroom, and her clothing was beside the bed. She was just gone.

"Maybe she went for a jog?" John thought to himself. **"It's six a.m. Who the hell goes for a jog by themselves at this time? You do."**

He was trying to make some sense out of this.

"She's gone." The house whispered.
"We have her now."
"You can't get her back."
"Gone forever."
"You her lost her again."
"This time for good."

The voices in the house were getting louder.

Abaddon

They were now laughing at him. Their voices and laughter filled every room and hallway, and it was deafening. He clamped down on his ears, but it did not stop the voices from entering his mind.

He heard a knocking sound and uncovered his ears. The knocking sound came again. It was the front door.

"Shit, the priest," John said out loud.

He went to the door; the senseless chatter that once filled the house's halls was gone. It was silent now, with no more laughter and nothing but the sound of John breathing and walking toward the door.

"Father Johnson, come on in."
"Good morning, John. Are you doing alright?"
"I'm fine, yeah, I'm fine. Why? Your priest senses tingling? Come on in."
"You look like shit."
"Well, thanks, Father. Aren't you priests not supposed to swear?"
"I told you, I'm not that kind of priest."

The priest entered the house and looked around it from the entryway, observing and seeing if anything unusual was happening.

"So, John, what's going on here?"
"What do you mean?"
"I feel a lot of oppression walking in here."
"I don't know what is going on here. That's why I am talking to you."

"Well, there is truth to that. Let's see what is going on here. Do you mind if I walk around?"
"Go right ahead, sorry if I don't buy into all this crap."
"It's fine. I didn't either."
"What made you change your mind?"
"I lost something significant, then found it. But it is more where I found it that changed me."
"Where and what did you find... well find it?"
"My wife, it's a long story, but I had to go to hell to find her again."
"What?" John said while laughing a little.
"Yup. I know... 'I would walk through hell for you.' Isn't that what we all say? Guess I had to prove it."
"You want me to believe that you actually went to hell."
"You believe what you want to. You asked me. I answered."

The priest walked throughout the first level of this house, then moved onto the second level.

"Where is she?"
"Who?"
"Caroline."
"I don't know."
"Meaning?"
"Meaning she wasn't in bed when I woke up. And I have no idea where she is."
"They took her, didn't they? You are going to have to go get her if you want her back."
"Go where? I don't know where to go."
"You know where."

Abaddon

"Don't tell me hell. I am not sure hell is real."
"You will find out. If you want her back."
"Of course, I want her back."
"Well then, let's get ready for the ride of our life."
"And what is that supposed to mean?"
"You will see."

John was stunned at the way this priest was talking. It was nothing like how he thought a priest would act: average, not judgmental, not all high and mighty. He seemed down to earth. This was the type of priest he could get used to.
But hell? What was he talking about?

"So, how am I supposed to get to hell? Aren't we already there?"
"Well, yes. But no. I am talking about the hell you have read about or may have been told about as a child. You said you were brought up Catholic, right?"
"Yes, I was."
"That hell. The fire, the pain, the darkness."
"So how do I get there?"
"Are you eager to go to hell?" Father Johnson laughed. I can help you; the door is in this house now. I will help you find it and prepare for this. It is not something to do blindly. You could get lost there and be stuck there. We don't want that. Trust me, you do not want to be stuck there."

The priest gave John some information to read and some prayers to practice—ways to prepare for this excursion.

"I will come back in a few days. We can start working then. Keep track of everything that happens here,

Abaddon

John; you must take note of everything, every whisper. Got it?"
"Like, in writing? Or what?"
"That might be helpful. Yes, journal everything. Even draw pictures if you have to. That dream you told me about, if you haven't written it down yet, I would."
"Why write this all down?"
"It will help you remember the small details. Those details might help you."
"I am not sure I will ever forget that dream."
"Good, still write everything down. And don't go back to your house. Just stay here at this house."
"I never mentioned owning another house."
"I know. This is why I am not your normal priest, my dear boy. I see things still, I hear things, I know things."
"Now you are just sounding like you're trying to be all mystical and Hollywood."
"If I was trying to sound or be Hollywood, I was do some dumb shit, like hand you an old-looking bottle of water and call it holly water, or maybe rosary beads. How about a crucifix? Would you like one of those? Maybe I could walk around with that stupid purple sash. Would you like that?"
"No, you're good, Father."
"Call me Andrew; this 'Father' stuff is getting old. Makes me feel old, too."

Abaddon

Abaddon

Chapter 9

John wasn't ready to dive into this type of thing. He still wasn't sure whether he believed in it.

The demons had been very active since Andrew got there this morning. They seemed agitated by his presence, which seemed odd to John based on their lack of reaction to him the other day. What made this time so different? Why were they actively trying to sway the two men?

"So, this is normal to you?" John asked Andrew.
"I wouldn't call this 'normal' if I'm being honest with you."
"What would you call it then, Father... I mean, Andrew?"
"Messed up. Now, are you ready? This is not to be taken lightly. You have to be ready. I have a question for you."
"Yes, I'm ready; what's your question."
"Do you want her back? Do you love this Caroline woman?"
"Yes, I love her. I would walk through Heaven and hell for her."
"I hope you mean that. Cause you might have to do that. Do you have the blanket from your dream?"
"Right here."

Abaddon

John pulled up the blanket that his mother had knitted before she passed. She used to love knitting blankets and things for people, but that all stopped when she was diagnosed with stage four cancer. This blanket was something John had held onto for years prior to passing. But now, it had been showing up repetitively in his dreams—the dreams he had been having of Caroline being taken by someone or something. This dream is the same one he had the night she disappeared and every night since.

"You are remembering the dream, correct?" The Father asked John.
"Yes, I am. I told you I may never get away from this dream."
"Good. But a simple "yes" or "no" will be fine. Now, which room did you see her disappear in?"
"One that is not in this house."
"Which room entered or connected to it?"
"The living room. Every room took me to it. But I got to it from the hall."
"Okay, so the hall outside this room would work. Here, drink this."

Andrew handed John a small glass, John took it and put it to his lips as to take a drink.

"What is it?"
"Just drink it."
"It smells like shit."
"Just drink it; you are better off not knowing what is in it."

Abaddon

John drank what was in the glass. He almost couldn't keep it down.

"That tastes like ass."
"I don't even want to know how you know what that even tastes like. Now relax, and we wait."

The Father began to pray a little prayer, which was calming for him. As he prayed, the growling in the house got louder. The storm was coming in fast, with lightning and thunder clapping outside.

"Leave Father. You cannot help him; she is ours."
"Ah, that voice sounds familiar. Sam, is that you? I remember you."
"You think you understand, don't you?"
"What is there to understand, Sam? You are doing it again. You will not win."
"This time, we will. We will kill her if we have to."
"You said that last time, but it was just you. Who is this we? Are you not working alone, Sam? Who are you working with this time?"
"Me. Us. All of us." A booming dark voice said.
"And who is us?"
"You father might know us as Legion."
"Oh, Legion, you say. Well, I am glad you have company."
"You still have jokes, I see, Father. I'm not sure you will be laughing when we kill her. John cannot and will never be happy again."
"Why not?"
"That is for us to know, not you. Those are our orders."

Abaddon

"So, you are still not strong enough to do it alone. You still need to be told what to do. Who's pulling your strings this time."
"You are playing with something that you cannot handle, Andrew, you got your whore back, but this one is ours. Now leave."
"I know you are afraid of my demon."
"We don't fear you, pathetic humans. Especially not you fucking priests."

John was now in a trans. Andrew turned to him, stopping his conversation with the demons. John was to be the focus, not the demons.

"John, can you hear me?" Andrew asked.
"Yes." He replied.
"Okay, good. Now, take the blanket. Try to find Caroline in the room she was taken."

John got up from the bed and sat on the corner. He grabbed the blanket his mom had knit, stood up, and walked toward the bedroom door. Andrew followed him. The house was now filled with the sound of the demons hissing and growling, trying to distract John from hearing the instructions Andrew was giving him. As John walked the halls of the house, Andrew followed. They came to a door.

"What is this door, John?"
"It's where she was."
"Caroline?"
"And Lilith."
"Together? John, was Lilith the one who took Caroline in your dream?"

Abaddon

"I think so."
"Go ahead, open the door," Andrew said as he waited for John to open it.

John reached for the doorknob, twisted it, and the door opened. To Andrew's surprise, it was just an empty room. John walked in, followed by Andrew. There was no sign of anything in the room but dust and a large armoire. Andrew was prepared for the door to open to something different; he thought it would open to hell. Something had happened in this room, but he had no idea what. Only John knew where to go next.

Andrew watched as John walked over to the armoire. As Andrew approached the armoire, the stench in the air became almost overwhelming. The smell of death and sulfur began to fill his lungs.

"Open it, John." The priest said softly.

As John opened the door, Andrew prepared himself to be face-to-face with hell once more. As John began to pull the door open, nothing but darkness appeared. Once opened, all that could be seen were the shelves of the old armoire. Andrew did not notice the puddle of blood behind him forming on the floor where John had first seen Lilith eating the baby. As he repositioned himself in the room, he almost slipped in the blood.

"This is where she took Caroline," John said as he pointed to the inside of the armoire.
"Then what happened, John?"
"The door shut."
"Then what, John?"

Abaddon

"I opened it, and she was gone."
"You have to enter it then," Andrew said.

Holding onto the red blanket, John started slowly stepping into the armoire. Then, shut the door. Andrew waited a moment before opening the door himself. Once he did, John was gone. Only the blanket remained.

Chapter 10

John stood in the pitch-black darkness, listening to the sounds around him. He could not see anything, only the echo of emptiness. He looked all over until he was able to see a light.

"*Father Johnson?*" He called out. "*Andrew. Can you hear me? Are you here?*"
"*I hear you, John.*"
"*Where are you? I can't see anything but some light in the distance. It's too dark.*"
"*I'm still in the room.*"
"*How can you hear me then?*"
"*I don't know. I hear you in the walls. Or maybe the air. Walk toward the light.*"
"*I'm dead?*"
"*I don't think you are, why?*"
"*You just told me to walk toward the light. Is that heaven?*"
"*Why are you asking me? I'm not there. Tell me what you see around you.*"
"*Nothing, it is too dark. You are the worst priest I have ever met.*"
"*Thank you?*" Father Johnson said sarcastically.
"*You don't even know what heaven looks like.*"
"*Heaven and hell are different for everyone. What I saw in heaven or hell might differ from what you see.*"

"Then what help are you? No offense."
"I've been through it. Some things are the same. They will manifest differently for each person. Besides, you said you would walk through heaven and hell for Caroline."
"I did say that, didn't I."
"Now, keep talking to me. I can hear everything you say. I am here to do everything I can."
"You going to pray for Johny boy, Father?" An ominous voice interrupted.
"If need be, but who do we have the pleasure of speaking to?"
"Oh, come on now, Father, if you know my name, then you have some sort of power against me."
"Then stop interrupting."
"Fuck you, Father. You are in my world now."
"Oh, 'Your world.' Let me guess, we are speaking with Satan now."
"I forgot. You are the great Father Johnson. You have been here before."
"I'm guessing you're not going to tell me who I am speaking to."
"I don't do what little priests tell me to. I am in charge."
"In charge, you say. You need to remember that I was there and got out. I even took my love with me."
"Not this time, you filthy priest. I am worse than Satan."
"I doubt that."
"Doubt all you want."
"Who are you, demon?"
"I am no mere demon." The voice laughed.

Abaddon

"If you are worse than the Prince of Darkness, tell me who you are. I want to know who we are dealing with."
"I am the one Satan fears; I am both friends with Heaven and Hell. Satan cannot destroy me."
"Abaddon, you are Abaddon."
"You are smart, Andrew."
"You have no idea."
"Father, I am getting close to the light. God, it stinks in here. So, umm… I kind of need you to stop the pissing contest with what's his face there and focus on helping me."
"What do you see?"

John explained what he was seeing in the light. The bright light filling his eyes was blinding. He saw something familiar in the distance.

"But it is my mother. She died years ago. This has to be Heaven."
"Now hold on, John. This could be a trick. They play a lot of tricks on your mind in hell, and remember, everyone's hell is different."
"But how could my mom be used against me in hell?"
"That I don't know."

As John exited the darkness, he found himself in a field with trees, a bright blue sky, and not a cloud in sight. In the distance, he noticed animals gathered and strolling around the fields. The sun was warm on his skin. He turned around to see where he had just come from, and there was nothing but more fields and trees. It was as if the dark tunnel he was just

Abaddon

in never existed. He continued to look around the landscape before him, surveying or taking it all in.

John approached the woman standing under a tree. She did not appear lost but content with her surroundings.

"Mom. Mom, is that you?" John asked.

She did not respond to him, as if she did not hear him. She turned her back toward John. As he approached her, he reached out to her shoulder. As he touched her, she spun around. John stumbled back in shock or maybe fear. He could not believe what he saw before him. This was no longer his mom.

It looked like his mom, but not. Her eyes were gone, just black pits, blood oozing from the eye sockets. The left side of her face was rotting away; her teeth were decaying, yellow, and covered in blood. She had blood dripping out of her mouth.

"Oh, my boy, what are you doing here?" She said to John. Her voice was a mixture of whispering and growling.
"What are you?"
"I'm your mother."
"Get away from me. You're not my mother." John snapped at her.
"Don't you want to hug you're Mother, John?"
"No, you're not my mother. What are you?"

In the blink of an eye, she pounced on top of John. He was on the ground, on his back. The blood from her face was falling on him.

Abaddon

"Come on, John. Give mommy a kiss."

Her fingernails were scratching him, and now she was digging them into his skin. He was struggling to push her off of him and break free.

"Don't you love your mommy?"

The more he struggled, the more she fought back. She started going in for a kiss, blood oozing from her mouth and falling on John's face. She had him pinned to the ground and was straddling him.

"Now come here and give Mommy some love. Do you not think I'm pretty?" Her voice was deeper now.

John saw the horns coming out of her skull, not uncovered by her hair. John is still struggling to get her off of him. He was filled with fear. He was in a flight or fight situation. All he wanted to do was get free and run. She grabbed him by the face.

"Listen Johny Boy. Give mommy a kiss. You love your mommy and want her to be proud of you, right? I can smell your fear. It makes me feel so good. Don't you want Mommy to feel good? Now come here and give me that kiss."

He finally mustered up the strength to roll her off of him just in time. She was inches away from kissing him. John got up off the ground, riddled with fear and disgust.

Abaddon

"Oh, John, you know I like it rough. Do it again." She laughed. *"Get rough with me, John. I'll even let you pull my hair. I've been very bad since I left Earth. You can punish me. I like to be punished. Come back."* She continued to laugh as she called out to him. Her voice was deep and dark, like a growling beast.

As John walked away, he could hear her laughing. Out of the corner of his eyes, he noticed the animal he had seen earlier. It was rotting as well. The animals were not complete; their bodies were disfigured and missing flesh. They were eating each other while still alive, gnawing at each other's flesh but not attacking each other. John turned his head away, looking forward again as he continued to walk away. John's ribs and neck were not bleeding; his shirt was ripped from the interaction with what he thought was his mother.

Chapter 11

"John?" Andrew called out as he sat in the living room of the house.

The storm outside was still there, blowing as if to rip the roof off. Andrew noticed that the storm was getting stronger. Branches were starting to break off the trees as the wind blew. The lightning illuminated the house every time it flashed.

"John, can you still hear me? What is going on?"
"Andrew," John replied, his voice seemingly coming out of thin air.
"Ok, you're still there. Good. Have you figured out if you are in Heaven or Hell?"
"After that, I am guessing Hell."
"After what?"
"That was not my mother. And those animals? Andrew, they were eating each other, yet they were still alive."
"The demons are playing off your memories now. They are going to keep doing that. Your wants and your dreams are only going to get worse from here, John. So, stay focused. Try not to interact with anyone or anything there."
"I don't know about worse, but I'll take your word."
"You don't have a lot of time. It would be best if you found Caroline."

Abaddon

"You don't think I'm working on that?"
"You have been in there for ten minutes, and you have already been attacked."
"Ten minutes? By my watch, it's been about five."
"Time works differently there. Just stay calm, and don't get angry. They feed off fear and anger. Well, anything negative. Look for another door or entry."
"Hold on, there is a house."
"Go to it and see."

    It was strange to John that a house that looked like his project home was in the middle of this field. He kept walking toward the house. As he got closer, he noticed something flying around it in the sky. The sky above the house was a fiery orange color. The door was not locked, so John opened the front door to it.
    As John entered, the air was cold and stale. He heard a noise coming from the second floor. As he walked up to the second floor, the noise got louder; it sounded like a bunch of women laughing. It was coming from the master bedroom.

"I'm coming up to the bedroom. That is where the noise is coming from."
"Just be careful, John."

    As John opened the bedroom door, to his amazement, she was there.

"Caroline? Is that you?"

    Andrew heard this and ran up to the bedroom. Caroline was there. Lying in bed asleep. Andrew pulled a chair up next to the bed and sat down.

Abaddon

"Get her out of there, John. You need to get her out. She is in bed here, but you can't leave her there."
"Got it."

John went over to Caroline to see if she would talk to him or even recognize him. This seemed to agitate the other women in the room or the demons. As John took Caroline out of the room to leave the house, they tried to stop him. They ran after him, reaching for them and clawing at them.

"You can't take her, John. She is ours. Just come and be with us. Stay."
"Don't listen to them, John; get out of there now."

The demons started to slow down and focus on the sound of Andrews's voice.

"She is ours, Priest."
"You don't get to keep her," **Andrew responded.**

He sat in the room Next to Caroline's sleeping body. He began to pray out loud.

"O God, you are the preserver of men and the keeper of our lives. We commit ourselves to your perfect care on the journey that awaits us. We pray for a safe and promising journey. Give Your angels charge over us to keep us in all our ways. Let no evil befall us, nor any harm come to our dwelling that we leave behind. Although we are uncertain what the days may bring, may we be prepared for any event or delay and greet such with patience and understanding. Bless us O

Abaddon

Lord, that we may complete our journey safely and successfully under Your ever watchful care."
"Stop it, priest; it won't work."
"Spirit of our God, Father, Son and Holy Spirit, Most Holy Trinity, Immaculate Virgin Mary, angels, archangels, and saints of heaven, descend upon me. Please purify me, Lord, mold me, fill me with yourself, use me. Banish all the forces of evil from me, destroy them, defeat them, so that I can be healthy and do good deeds. Banish from me all spells, witchcraft, black magic, evil spells, ties, curses, and the evil eye; diabolic infestations, oppressions, possessions; all that is evil and sinful, jealousy, deceitfulness, envy; physical, psychological, moral, spiritual and diabolical ailments. Burn all these evils in hell, that they may never again touch me or any other creature in the entire world. I command and bid all the powers who molest me—by the power of God, all-powerful, in the name of Jesus Christ our Savior. Through the intercession of the Immaculate Virgin Mary–to leave me forever, and to be consigned into the everlasting hell where they will be bound by Saint Michael the archangel, Saint Gabriel, Saint Raphael, our guardian angels, and where they will be crushed under the heel of the Immaculate Virgin Mary."

    John opened the house's front door and was in the empty room with the armoire. He slammed the door shut to the armoire and noticed Caroline was not with him. He looked at the floor in sheer disappointment. He felt as though he had failed. She was not there; he didn't notice her letting go of his hand. He had lost her forever.
    He felt so weak at this moment. He noticed the blood stain on the floor, which had started to dry. He walked to the

door and opened it to leave. Exiting the room, he noticed the chill in the air again. The storm outside was horrible; the lightning flashed. The lights in the house were all off.

As he walked by his bedroom, he saw the light under the door. He heard Andrew praying. John entered the room and saw Caroline in the bed. He ran to her side, excited to see her back in the house.

> *"Lord Jesus, I come before you in faith, acknowledging the power and significance of your precious blood. I plead the covering of your blood over me and my loved ones, from the crown of our heads to the soles of our feet. By the power of your blood, I renounce every form of evil, sin, temptation, and affliction that seeks to harm us. I break off and tear down every stronghold and power of darkness. Lord, fill us with your Holy Spirit and protect us from all harm and danger. I thank you, Jesus, for shedding every drop of your precious blood to redeem us and set us free from the clutches of Satan. I trust in the power of your blood to shield us and keep us safe from all evil influences. May the blood of Jesus be a fortress around us, guarding us from all forms of spiritual attack. Cover us with your divine protection and grant us peace and security in your loving embrace. In your mighty name, Jesus, I pray. Amen."*

Father Johnson finished his prayer.
"Is it over now?" John asked.
"I don't know. Only time will tell," Andrew said.
"What do you mean by that?"
"We have to wait. It took days for my wife to come back. Basically, we are waiting for her to come out of a coma."
"Ok? So, what do I do until she wakes up?"
"Can you cook?"

Abaddon

"Yes, but what does that have to do with anything?"
"I'm going to stay here, just in case, and I get hungry. But I will be here, and I will be praying over her. You need to keep going on with your life."
"She is my life."
"You know what I mean. Do your usual thing, whatever it is you do. Go to work and all that."

Caroline was lying still in bed that night. Her body was as stiff as a board. She looked lifeless. Andrew reached over with a rag to wipe away the sweat. She had been running a fever for hours.

Her eyes snapped open. They were as red as blood. Huge black bags surrounded her eyes. Her veins could be seen through her skin as if her skin were glass. She grabbed his wrist as he tried to back away from her. His skin started to burn where she was holding him, and in an instant, she snapped his wrist. He let out a yell from the unbearable pain as his bones broke. John had left the room to get a drink from the kitchen, and when he heard Andrew, he dropped the glass on the floor and ran up the stairs to the room.

"What happened?" John asked as he burst into the room.

Then John saw Caroline sitting up in the bed.

"Don't make eye contact," Andrew said.
"What the hell is she doing?"

Caroline was gyrating in the bed, drooling and panting like a dog.

"You like what you see, Johnny Boy?"
"Don't talk to it."

Abaddon

"It you mean her."
"I mean it. That voice is not Caroline."
"Oh, is this where we go all Catholic? Start splashing Holy Water on her."
"It might come to that. But for now, do not talk to it. It will try to convince you it is Caroline and that she needs your help, but we already know she needs your help, and you are giving her help. Just don't fall for the Hollywood tricks."
"Oh, Father. You are no fun. How about you boys get in bed with me? We can have some fun together."

She started to undress herself; Andrew turned his head that other way and continued to nurse his wrist.

"Oh, come on, Father Johnson. You can look. I'll even let you touch. You know you want to; I can see it in you."

John grabbed a blanket and covered her bare body. As time passed, she was becoming more aggressive toward Andrew and John. It was late, and the two men were getting tired. They finished securing Caroline to the bed so she would not hurt herself or the two of them.

John went to one of the guest rooms he had set up to call it a night. He couldn't help it, but every time he closed his eyes, he was met by images of the woman from his dream—the one who had taken Caroline away.

Abaddon

Abaddon

Chapter 12

He jumped out of bed from a deep slumber. Caroline's screaming, which sounded like she was in pain, woke him. He ran to the room to see what was going on. Andrew was already in the room. Caroline was thrashing her body around in bed, growling and screaming. Some of the most fowl things John had ever heard came out of her mouth.

"Why is she 'panting' like that?"
"When a demon enters your body, it kind of restricts your breathing ability."
"Oh, wow, I had no clue."
"Same here. No, I have no clue why that happens."
"So, you have no clue what is going on. Yet you are going to save the life of my love?"
"Come on now, boys. Fight nicely." Caroline said in a sultry voice.
"Nope. Sorry to say this, John, but you are still looking at this like some movie."
"Well, I'm not trained in all this. You are. Do the exorcism thing."
"Oh, now that sounds fun, John. Andrew, why don't you tell him about the last time you did one of those? Tell John all about it. Tell him what happened to the little girl. Such an innocent little thing she was. Her funeral was beautiful; all the flowers were so pretty. Everyone crying, all the tears." Caroline laughed while she spoke.

Abaddon

"What is she talking about, Andrew?"
"Pay her no attention," Andrew responded avoidantly.
"Did something happen, Andrew? Tell me what happened."
"It's not like in the movies, John. Some of them don't want to be saved. Some of them resist. God gives us that choice. He gives us free will."
"What are you saying?"
"I lost her, ok? She passed. My first exorcism was not a success."

John looked at Andrew, shocked. He could not believe what he had just heard come out of Andrew's mouth.

"You lost her? Meaning?"
"Meaning she died," Andrew replied in a somber tone.

John was instantly filled with concern at this point. What if his Caroline were to die due to all of this? What would he do with himself? How would he move on? He was standing there gazing off to space with a blank look. All he had ever wanted, what he had fought for so hard with others, was right there before him.

"John. JOHN." Andrew shouted at him.
"Huh…" John replied slowly, shaking his head.
"John, listen. I need you here and focused. Caroline needs you here."
"You're right. I need to focus on what is in front of me."

Abaddon

It was very late, and it was dark outside. The rain was coming down gently, but the lightning was getting more frequent, lighting up the night sky at every flash. Caroline appeared to be asleep at the moment. Father Johnson was feverishly praying over her, and John had been sitting across the bed from him. Andrew's wrist was tightly wrapped where Caroline had broken it earlier.

John stood up and started walking to the window to look outside. He needed to wake himself up but did not want to leave Andrew alone. As he stood by the window, the storm worsened. He noticed something, something that did not sit well with him.

"...amen."
"Andrew."
"Yes, John, what is it?"
"Come here. Quickly. There is something you need to see."

Andrew got up and walked over to John and the window.

"What is it?" He asked as he approached John.
"Do you see them?"
"See who?"
"That," John said as he pointed to the sky.

At that moment, the lightning flashed, and the sky lit up. The men looked at the sky in amazement. They could not believe what they saw. The Sky was filled with figures circling his house and starting to descend upon it. The two men were quickly interrupted by a deep, ominous voice. It was coming from Caroline.

"Come and get me, boys. You think you can take me? You will watch your friend's bleed. You cannot stop me. I will bathe in your blood. You pathetic pieces of shit. Worshipping your god. Do you want to come for us? Well, come on, we will make you pay for this and show you who you should be bowing to. Our brothers and sisters are coming to join us. Once they get in here, you and your precious little Caroline will never be together."

When the men turned to see her, she stood on the bed, her arms stretched out, looking toward the sky. She had blood rolling down her body from her head, and her hair was saturated in blood. Her nails were long and black, and her skin was pale white. She had scratched down her arms, which hadn't been there prior.

"Get my bag, would you, John? It's over there."
Andrew pointed toward the door of the room.

John did as he was asked. As he picked up the bag, he heard a hypnotic whisper calling to him.

"Andrew, do you hear that?"
"Hear what?"
"That voice."
"I don't hear anything."
"I must be going crazy."
"That's right, John, you're simply going crazy. Why don't you check it out and see what they want? Maybe you can save them or not. You never know till you go check. They need your help. Help them. Or maybe you

Abaddon

are too scared to leave your boyfriend, Andrew. Don't worry about Caroline; we've got her. She will be safe with all of us. She is going to love my brothers. Oh, the things we are going to do to her and her body. We can all take turns showing her what it will be like to feel a real man. She will never want you again, John."
"Shut the hell up," John shouted in anger.
"Oh, did we strike a nerve, John? Do you not want her body taken by us? How about her life? Do you want us to take her life instead?"
"You aren't going to do anything to Caroline."
"Little human. Insignificant mortal. You don't understand, do you?"
"I understand that if you don't leave her right now, you will not like the wrath Andrew, and I will bring to you."
"You think you and that failure can do anything to us. You don't even understand what is going on. You and the priest are nothing to us."
"I don't know what is going on, I don't know who or what you are, and I don't care. I love Caroline, and you are not going to do anything to her over my dead body."
"Yes, John, your dead body will be nice. We will surely kill you if you try to fuck with us." A new voice said.
"He doesn't get it." Another voice laughed.
"He doesn't understand." More voices started coming out of Caroline.

Abaddon

John was very frustrated and scared, and it was showing. His fists were clenched by his side. He started toward Caroline, but Andrew quickly held him back.

> *"John, I need you to stay calm; Caroline is going to need you to be focused here. I think we might need to go out of the room for a bit. Take a breather."*

John was breathing heavily as he pushed forward, fighting against Andrew to get to Caroline. Andrew held John back, nudging him toward the door. John nodded, and the two men stepped out of the room. As they were leaving, Andrew quickly bent down, grabbed his bag, exited the room after John, and shut the door.

Chapter 13

"I hope you are getting all this," Abaddon told Paige. *"Yes, yes, I am,"* Paige replied as she checked the recorder. *"How do you know all of this happened?"*
"I was there. I watched everything unfold from day one. I was in the room watching the demons control this young lady."
"You mean possess her. Right?"
"No. I mean, control her, influence her. See, these little demons could not possess her. She had too much beauty, love, and hope inside her."
"Why not go after John and possess him? He was struggling with his beliefs and relationship with God, as they say."
"Remember, she was the target for Mother, not John. So, we could not do anything to him."
"And you had to do what she said?"
"Yes. She had a pact with Satan; he gave her control."
"So, what did John see outside his house that night?"
"Well, that is easy, my dear Paige. Those were angels and demons. They were coming to remove the demons trying to attack John and Caroline. I guess that priest was praying for help. And he got it."
"Now you were saying the demons were not possessing Caroline but controlling her. What do you mean by that?"

Abaddon

"So, as I said, young Paige. She was too full of hope and love. She was not weak enough. Plus, how should I put this? She was a little bit of a witch herself. She was all about crystals and good energy, that type of thing. Plus, her love was so real when it came to John; that is something demons don't like, and as weak as those demons were, they could not battle it. So, essentially, she was too pure and good-hearted. Plus, those putrid little demons were unable to break her down. They knew they would not be able to impact John, for the reason I stated before, so they used Caroline as a puppet. Pulling at her strings. If Mother had just sent me in, I would have taken care of this a lot quicker."
"Why you?"
"Because, at that time, I was not swayed by love. I was to the point; I always got the job done right."
"What do you mean by that?"
"By what?"
"You said '... at the time...' Did something change?"
"Yes, something did change. Being in this human body has made me see things differently. Before this, I had never been or felt like being attached to anyone. I saw the love John had for Caroline. The things he was willing to do to save her. This was intriguing to me. I have heard men say over and over that they would walk through heaven or hell to save their love. The first man I saw doing this was Andrew, and the second was John. They both had such a deep love for their partner that they went to heaven and then hell to save them. I could not understand it. Why would they do this? When Mother told me to focus on John, and I witnessed him do this for Caroline, I started to watch

Abaddon

him, as well as I saw her fighting to get to John. That started to change something inside of me."

Abaddon stopped talking for a moment. He sat in the chair, staring at the roaring fire. He had an empty glass in his hand. He got up for the first time that evening. He was well over six feet tall, with long black hair past his shoulders. He stood up very straight, not slouched over at all. He walked over to a bar table against the wall and grabbed a bottle to pour himself another drink.

"You were talking about John and Andrew leaving the room?"
"Yes, I was talking about that night."

As he walked back to his chair, he entered the light of the fire. His eyes were black as night. He strolled toward the chair, drink in hand, then slowly lowered himself into a relaxing position.

"So, I was speaking of that night. It was a brutal battle outside. I never got involved with those things; then, I would have to pick a side, which I wouldn't. That is not what He made me for."
"What things?"
"The fights between angels and demons. The stench of demons bleeding was permeating the air. They were fighting outside. The angels were trying to stop the demons from entering the house."
"So, God sent them to do that?"
"Who knows what God does?"
"Tell me about this priest; what was so important about him?"

Abaddon

"Ah, yes, the priest. God marked him. He was the first to travel into hell as a living being and back to this life from hell safely."
"Marked by God?"
"Yes. God marked his heart and soul. He usually would assign an angel of protection to you humans. One that guides you through your time on earth and protects you. A guardian angel. But Andrew was protected by God. Why, you might ask. I do not understand why God does what He does. But He has His reasons. He does not tell all of us why He does it. He is God. He does what He wants. Let me continue my story where I left off. The two men were in the hallway outside the bedroom door."

Chapter 14

"What the hell is going on in there Andrew?" John demanded.
"Let's go make some coffee, shall we?" Andrew said as he walked toward the stairs. *"Yes, I think we need coffee and a snack."*

The two men walked downstairs to the kitchen, where John made them some coffee. They sat at the round wooden table in the kitchen.

"Why is this happening to her, Andrew? Why us?"
"From the outside looking in. I couldn't tell you."
"What can you tell me? You showed up on my doorstep right when this shit was happening. Why?"
"Tell me more about you and Caroline."
"Well, we met a few years ago and took a shot at a relationship. I wasn't the best man to be in a relationship with. She called it off at one point, but then she came back. We decided to throw caution to the wind, finish this place, sell it, and live together. I just can't understand any of this."
"So, you loved her, did you?"
"More than anything, I don't even think that love is a strong enough word to explain how I feel about her. The connection I feel with her is indescribable to me. But with what happened last time..., I was shocked she came back. I can't lose her again. I don't know

Abaddon

what I would do if she left me again. This is like a second chance for me to feel alive again, not that I have never felt alive before. But this is different. It feels odd to say, but I feel like her coming back into my life is truly a blessing from God."

"It was God giving you a gift. You are very important to Him."

"Yes, I know 'We are all God's children...' I heard it all in Sunday School and Church as a kid. But look at my past. Nothing ever went right. After my second divorce, my life seemed to crash. Caroline left me when I needed her most."

"First off, John, you are special to God. No, it is not just the Sunday School phrase being used. I know He has marked you. And what is so special about your second divorce? What happened?"

"Nothing seemed to have happened. Like I didn't get sick or in an accident or anything. I lost everything after that divorce, not in the divorce or because of the law. No, nothing like that. I just emotionally seemed to lose control of everything. I lost two jobs back-to-back. But then Caroline came into my life. Things weren't perfect in my life, but they were getting better. It went from constant lows to major peaks and valleys. I am sure I know for a fact that it had to be rough on her. If I could just work harder or faster at getting things under control, I would have been able to 'keep' her in my life. But I couldn't do it. Since the divorce, I have always felt like something or someone was watching me. Controlling the things around me to act, not in my favor." John stopped for a moment, a glimmer of hope in his eyes. "I sound *paranoid, don't I?"*

Abaddon

"No, you don't," Andrew replied, listening intently to every word.
"At the start of our seeing each other, it was great; toward the end, I started having the feeling that I would never have anyone or anything nice in my life like someone was stopping me from being able to be happy. I went to therapy because I felt like it had to be me from stopping myself, as in myself."
"What next?"
"I started feeling like someone was there again, watching me and controlling my environment."
"Who do you think that was? Why would they do it to you, John?"
"I'd love just to go the easy route and blame my ex because she always seemed to know what I was doing when I was about to do it. I was like she had someone following me or watching me constantly and reporting intel back to her. But that is when Caroline left me. That is when she called off the relationship. She said it was best for us; she just wanted me to be happy and stop holding myself back."
"What if I told you that you were not wrong?"
Andrew responded.
"Whatever. That is just me speaking as a scorned ex-husband, I think."
"Is it, John? What happened when Caroline left you? Did things start easing up for you?"
"Yes, as a matter of fact, things did start getting better, not because Caroline was not in my life anymore. But when she came back a few years later, I felt like I had achieved a higher level of happiness that was never available to me before."
"Who seemed to not be in your life as well?"

Abaddon

"Well, my ex-wife was leaving me alone," John answered with a puzzled look.
"But when Caroline returned, your ex-wife got angry, didn't she?"
"Seems like she did."
"Then all of this started happening. Want me to let you in on a little secret?"
"Let me guess; God told you this."
"You got that right, John. Something you need to know about me: when I went to 'save' my love that was taken from me, I saw God in heaven. He told me about you. He told me that I needed to find you and help you. He guided me to you directly."
"I am sure He did," John responded, being very sarcastic.
"Listen to me John. I don't care if you believe in God or not. You care about Caroline, right?"
"Clearly."
"Are you willing to do whatever it takes to get her back?"
"Yes."
"Then shut up and listen to me. God told me when and where to find you. The problem for me has been that I have had other things I needed to do. But you have been of great importance to me over the past six months."
"We just met a week ago."
"I told you. God told me about you a while back. I have been looking into you for quite some time. And you hop around a lot with your little house projects. God told me how to track you down better. He even assigned several of his angels to find you. When you

Abaddon

showed up here at this house, you really shook things up for us."
"How so? I don't understand."
"You bought this house to reconstruct it. This house was built on the battlefield of heaven and hell. It's a very long story, and we don't have time for the entire thing. We must save Caroline. But this location is where Satan and the demons will enter on Judgement Day. Under this house is the gate to the to hell."
"You want me to believe I own the house built on the gate to hell?"
"No. This is the gate to hell. You must understand this because it strengthens their hold on her. We will not get her back if we don't start acting fast. But my goal, my instructions from God, are to protect you."
"Why me? What is so important about me?"
"This one is going to be hard for you to accept."
"No bullshit Andrew, just say it to me. No long stories, just the truth."
"Okay, here I go. You, John, you are a direct descendant of Adam. That is why. That is why you are so important to God. Your ex-wife has been casting spells in your direction with the help of demons and Satan. That is about as straightforward and blunt as I can be."
"What?" John said while almost spitting out the drink he had just taken.
"I told you it was going to be hard for you to accept."
"Which part?" John said, chuckling.
"Both Parts, the entire thing. I mean, it sounds ludicrous to me as well."
"You want me to believe I am like the great, great, great, whatever grandson of Adam? The Adam. Like

the Garden of Eden Adam from the Bible. And, after that, you think I need to believe my ex-wife is at home making deals with Satan. Just to fuck with me?"
"It would make my job easier if you did."
"Oh, that's right 'you are on a mission from God' right."
"Yes, and not the way you mean it. You are not my mission. But at the same time, you are a part of my mission."
"Well, don't I feel special now? I am part of your mission. I am hurt; I'm not the complete mission." John said in a very sarcastic tone.
"Again, I understand your position. All I ask is that you trust me and follow my instructions. Can you do that? Can you put your sarcasm aside long enough to save Caroline? We need to not focus on your ex and her actions right now. We may have to deal with what she is doing. Not focus on what she is doing."
"I could and would do anything for her. I have told you that."
"Yes, you did. And to quote, 'you would walk through heaven and hell' to save her. I am assuming that is still the case, right? Even after your first trip to hell?"
"Yes, it is," John replied confidently.
"Then, it is time for you to put your sarcasm and disbelief aside."
"It's not that I don't believe."
"Whatever it is. Put it aside. Let's finish up her and check on her. Then we can begin to get her back."

The two men finished their drinks in the kitchen and returned to the room. Caroline was not there, and there were

Abaddon

no signs of her having been there. The bed was made as if it was in the morning. John checked the bed, feeling around for residual body heat or any sign that someone had been in it just minutes before.

John fell to his knees, visibly emotional about this. He started yelling at Andrew about how long they had been out of the room. He felt as though he had lost his love yet again. It was becoming overwhelming for him, the heartache and the pain. And we went to his side to console him.

> *"Why Andrew? Why does God keep doing this to me? Why, if I am so damn special and important, can I not have happiness in my life? Why is He not putting a stop to this and protecting me and my household?"*
> *"Hear me out, John. Please be open to this. God wants you to be happy and to feel love. But He needs you to do the work. He needs your help with this. He needs you to be stronger than this. We need to do some things now. You need to get yourself ready. We need to get some rest. There is nothing we can do right now. Okay?"*
> *John answered Andrew through the tears, "Okay."*
> *I will ask you to do things that will not make sense, but I need you to trust me and do what I ask of you."*
> *Again, John answered him, "Okay."*
> *"Okay, good. Now we need our rest."*

Andrew walked John to his room and helped him get into the bed. John quickly fell asleep.

> *"God, Speak to me now. Please. Lead me and guide me on this journey. John needs you to be in my ears.*

Abaddon

He needs your comfort as well. In your heavenly name, we pray. Amen!"

Chapter 15

John and Andrew were in the room with the armoire again. It was raining outside again, but it was more of a calming rain than a thunderstorm.

"I don't have to drink that shit you made last time again, do I?"
Andrew replied with a chuckle, *"Yes, here it is. Nice and fresh, just for you. Now up."*
"Don't quit your day job. Just stick to being a priest."
"Not sure I'm that good at being one of those either."

John took the cup from Andrew's hands and began to drink it. A few minutes passed; it seemed to work like last time. John stood up from the chair he was sitting in and walked toward the armoire, blanket in hand again. When he reached the armoire, he opened the door like last time, entered it, turned around, and shut the door.

John stood again in the pitch-black darkness, listening to the sounds around him. He began to look around to see if he could find the light he had once seen. This time, a prominent smell surrounded him, and it was unpleasant to breathe for John. He saw the light and began walking toward it. As he got closer to this gateway of light, he noticed that the air became fresher; the temperature was that of a fresh spring evening, and a slight breeze came to him. As he continued walking, he was in a field again. This time, he was greeted by many familiar faces and voices of his past. They seemed happy and excited to see him. His heart was filled with peace and joy like never before. This feeling of peace took everything in him.

As he was welcomed by everyone standing in the field, John noticed what appeared to be a man with long blond hair. This man had a glow surrounding him as if the sun was hiding behind him. His smile was very pleasant. He stood above the group of greeters as he was an exceptionally tall man. John and the man made eye contact.

"Hello, John. It is good to see you."
"Do I know you?" John replied.
"Yes and no. We have never met, but I have been watching you since birth. You have read about me a lot."
"Are you God?"
"No." The man responded and laughed.
"Then who are you, and how do we know each other?"
"I am your guardian angel, Michael. Yes, the Michael, from the Bible."
"Why would I have an archangel as a guardian angel?"
"The father wanted and needed you to be watched over. You are important to God, so He needed someone like me to watch over you." Michael said while smiling.
"But He let all those things happen to me. Why not protect me from it all?"
"You are still here, aren't you?"

Abaddon

"Yes, but look at all I have lost and what I might lose if I don't find Caroline."
"Well, we can't have that now, can we? Walk with me."

The two of them walked, talking the entire time.

"I can see that you love her. I can tell how much her life means to you, but are you ready to go through hell to find her?"
"Yes, I am. That is where I was trying to get to again."
"Yes, that is right. You have already been to hell with the help of Father Johnson. That is who helped you get here. So, you want to go there again?"
"It's not like I want to. But I am willing to for Caroline and her life. You don't get it, do you?"
"I do not have the kind of love you are talking about. But I understand what you mean, John. It is admirable of you to do anything you can for the woman you love. Does she know how much you desire her and what you are doing to save her?"
"I think so. I mean, I hope so."
"We shall see."
"I am not doing this for show. I am doing this because I love everything about her and do not want to go another second without her in my life."
"I don't want to slow you down then. Here we are."

Michael pointed toward a cave. John knew he would have to enter the cave to get where he needed to go. It was a large cave, not even at the bottom of a mountain or a hill. To John, it looked like a large boulder with an entry.

Abaddon

"Are you coming with me?"
"No, I am sorry. We can only be down there for specific reasons during specific times. You, my friend, will have to do this alone for Caroline. Goodbye, my friend. I will be with you when you return."

John said his goodbyes to Michael and began walking toward the cave. He was hit with a horrid smell when he entered the cave again. To him, it smelt like routing or decaying bodies and sulfur. He continued walking slowly, as there was little to no light. He heard noises that were chilling to the bones. It sounded like people screaming in pain, screams of terror. He saw an orange glow around a corner, so he headed that way toward the glow.

He was on the edge of an opening, looking down at thousands upon thousands of people being tortured. It seemed that the people were in pain of every type. He couldn't bear to look at this site anymore; he closed his eyes and turned his body away from it. The noise and screams disappeared. There was no longer any more screaming. He opened his eyes. He was in the house again. But it was different somehow. It was his house, but he felt he did not belong there. None of the work that he remembered having done was completed as he remembered. It looked like it did the day he bought it. As he passed the living room, he heard a deep, dark, and ominous voice speak to him. He froze in his footsteps.

"Hello John, it is good to see you are back. We can now finally meet."

John turned toward the voice in the living room. He noticed a man sitting in an oversized chair before the

Abaddon

fireplace. As John looked closer at the man, he saw that the right side of his face was decaying and had no skin on it. One of the horns protruding from the man's head had been broken off.

"Come closer, my boy. Or shall I come to you?"

John was still frozen at the moment. The man started to stand up from the chair and walked slowly toward John. He was an immense man with a limp, dragging his left leg as he came closer to John. John could not move; he wanted to run.

"I know why you are here. You can't have her."
"You can't stop me."

The man, now face-to-face with John, began to laugh at John as if John had just told the best joke in the world.

"I am not here to stop you. I am here to welcome you home. This is where you belong. By my side."
"This is not my home."
"But it can be. If you want her, you will have to stay. She is not going anywhere. You can't beat me. She is mine now, and I will not give her up."

Then, the man faded away in a mist, leaving John alone at the entry. John then heard a woman scream. It was Caroline's voice coming from upstairs. John ran up the stairs toward the room where her voice came from. As he burst through the door, the room was empty. He heard her calling for him to help her from down the hall. He exited the room and noticed a woman enter a room a few doors down from him. As he went to every room looking frantically for Caroline,

Abaddon

he found nothing but an empty room. As he exited the last room, he saw the women walking into another room again. He slowly walked to the last room. It was the room with the armoire in it. He entered the room cautiously and saw the woman sitting in a chair; her back was to him.

> *"You can't have her. He will not let you leave with her again. She is forever stuck here. He will kill you if you don't leave soon. He will keep you here for eternity."*
> *"You know where she is, don't you?"*
> *"Yes."*
> *"Tell me."*
> *"I can't. He will know. You would fail anyway."*
> *"Who will know?"*
> *"The one in charge."*
> *"And that would be?"*
> *"Stupid boy, Satan."*

John stood there in silence for a moment. Trying to take in everything he had heard and seen. Was he really dealing with demons or Satan? Was he really in hell having a conversation like this, or was it all in his head? Was this just a dream or a nightmare? Who was this woman in front of him, he wondered. She sounded familiar as if they had spoken before. His stomach was beginning to feel very uneasy at this moment. He started to walk further into the room toward her to see who she was. As he approached her, he began to walk around to see her from the front. He wanted to get a look at her face.

She was an older black lady. Frail in stature, she looked very aged. As he approached the front of her, he noticed her eyes were sealed shut. Her mouth had been sown

Abaddon

shut. It was the woman from his nightmares. He stumbled backward and almost slipped in a puddle of blood.

"What the fuck is she doing here?" John thought to himself.

She began to laugh, and her laugh got louder as the seconds passed. John needed clarification. How could she be talking to him and now laughing with her mouth shut? She was laughing so hard at this point that the thread that tied her mouth shut began ripping her lips and breaking. As the last portion of the thread broke, she could open her mouth.
John stood there in shock, his back against the wall. She turned her head to look at him. She stood up from the chair, looking at him. In an instant, she was in front of him. She grabbed him by the arms and held him against the wall; he could not break free of her grip.

"You stupid son of a bitch. You came here by yourself. You are too weak to do anything. I warned you in your dreams. I took Caroline away from you once. And I'm doing it again. You will never get her back. She does not love you. You are pathetic. We are going to feast off your soul. Then, when we are done with you, we will feast on hers. Go back, or you will die by our hands. Love is not going to help you. You will never have love."
"Get off of me, you crazy old bat," John said while struggling.
"I am going to rip your pretty little face off. Then I am going to eat your intestines while you are still breathing." She growled at him.

Abaddon

John, through all his frightened struggles, finally broke free of her. He shoved her to the ground and quickly backed away from her. She began laughing again at him. She started crawling toward him.

> *"I'm going to gut you like the little pig you are, John."*
> *"Andrew, Andrew, can you hear me?"* John began calling out.
> *"Yes, John, I can hear you. What's going on?"* Responded quickly.
> *"Yes, you little bitch. Talk to your friend. He can't do anything to help you."* The woman said as she advanced toward John.
> *"I need help, Andrew."*
> *"O St. Joseph, guardian and protector of the Holy Family, I come before you in humility and with trust, seeking your intercession and protection. You were entrusted with the sacred duty of safeguarding Jesus and Mary, and I implore you to extend your loving care over John…"* John could hear Andrew's prayer.

She grabbed John's ankle. He balled up his hand to make a fist and punched her in the face. He started to kick her as fast and hard as he could. Andrew continued to pray.

> *"St. Joseph, defender against evil and adversity, shield us from all harm and danger. Protect us from physical harm, emotional distress, and spiritual attacks. Help us to navigate the challenges and trials of life with strength, courage, and grace. Intercede for us, dear St. Joseph, that we may be granted the blessings of safety, security, and peace. Guide us in*

Abaddon

making wise decisions and lead us on the path of righteousness. May your loving presence surround us and keep us from all harm. St. Joseph, foster father of Jesus, pray for us now and at the hour of our death. Amen."

The woman's body was on the floor. She was no longer laughing or speaking. It did not look as though she was breathing. John went over to her body to check and see if she was still alive. He poked her, but she did not respond. She was dead.

"I think she is dead, Andrew."
"How do you know?"
"I don't. I poked her, and she did not respond. How can you tell if a dead person in hell is dead again?"
"Never mind that. You need to find Caroline."
"Right. I don't think she is in this house. I have looked everywhere."
"Can you hear anything or anyone?"
"I can hear her."
"Follow her voice."

John started to follow her cries for help. His voice echoed throughout the halls as he called for her to keep speaking so he could find her. Her voice got louder as he walked toward the first floor. He went down the staircase cautiously, listening intently to Caroline's sound. Her voice was coming from outside the house. As he approached the front door, he was filled again with the wafting stench of death in the air. He could see the dark clouds and lightning in the sky out the windows. He stretched his hand cautiously toward the door to open it. He felt the intense heat against his

Abaddon

skin as he opened the door. To his amazement, the sky was no longer dark once the door was opened.

Abaddon

Chapter 16

It was as if the door was a portal. What he had seen through the windows, a dark stormy night, was now a field of what looked to be wheat, swaying gently in the breeze. He was now standing in the field by himself. A dead tree was off in the distance, its branches reaching like skeletal fingers. A cool breeze was blowing across the field and through his hair. The air was silent; there was no audible sound to be heard. He noticed movement in the distance. It was Caroline. She was walking toward him. She seemed to be in some trans; she did not even notice John standing there. She smiled and waved to someone. John turned his head to look for an exit and see who she was waving at. He saw a tall figure behind him, standing still about thirty feet away. Caroline approached John and walked right past him. It was as if he was not there. She continued walking toward the other figure. At this moment, the figure turned to face John, his features shrouded in darkness.

The figure was now staring at John with a sinister smile, his eyes glinting with a malevolence that sent shivers down John's spine. Chills went down John's spine as he looked at the man, his heart pounding. It was the man or being from the living room, but now, in this strange field, he seemed even more menacing, more otherworldly.

"Caroline," John called to her.

Abaddon

The man responded to John, *"She is here for me, not you. I told you before, as others have, you can't have her. She is ours now."*
"Caroline, it's me. I'm here to take you back. I came here to get you."

She turned to him. She now had a confused look on her face.

"John?" She asked. *"Is that you? Why are you here? What are you doing?""*
"Yes, it's me. I am here for you. We can go back home together. Just come over here to me. Take my hand. We can go home now."
"I'm scared." She said.
"it's ok, I'm here. We got this this. Just come here, babe."

She started walking toward John. This angered the other man. He started walking toward John.

"Caroline, you need to come here now." The man ordered.

Caroline did as she was told. She stood next to him subserviently. He wrapped his arm around her, placing his hand on her shoulder. He leaned in closer to her and licked her face with his long black tongue as if to mark his territory.

"Mmm. The sweat taste of her flesh. Don't you miss it, John?" He said as he looked over at John.
"John, help me." She said with tears in her eyes.

Abaddon

"You cannot go with him, Caroline. Your home is here now."
"But I want to be with him."
"That cannot be my child. He does not care for you like we do. He does not love you like I do."

He held her tighter and closer to him.

"Help me, John." She said in a melancholy tone.

John did not see an exit nearby, and the house was nowhere to be seen in the field. He knew he had to do something, and he had to do it quickly. As she passed him, he grabbed Caroline by the hand, and they began running.

As they ran, the atmosphere around them began to change. They were no longer in a field but in the dimly lit streets of a housing development. It was no longer sunny; it was as if the sun instantly set and the moon came out, creating nighttime. There was a storm coming in. The thunder was loud, and the lightning was brightly and wildly lighting up the sky. John had no idea which way to go, so he continued running. Suddenly, the houses started looking familiar to him. John knew this was the neighborhood around the corner from the house.

"I know this place. I think I know where we are."
John said to Carolin with a tone of relief.
"Are we home? I want to go home."
"Home is around the corner; I am going to get us there, just trust me."
"Promise me."

Abaddon

John was not the type to make promises; things always happen when people make promises. But this was different for him; it was Caroline, and he knew he would get her home where she would be safe.

> *"I promise you, Caroline. I am going to get us home. I am going to fix this all and make it go away. I am not going to let anything hurt you."*

They turned left on the street and continued to run. At the end of the street was the entrance to the neighborhood. They turned right and headed to where the house was.

> *"I'm tired, John."* She said to him.
> "Not much further. Hang with me. We are almost there." John said while out of breath.
> *"I can't go any further."*

John looked at her. He knew they had to return, so he picked her up and carried her. He had about a mile left to walk to the house; he was sure he could get them back home there. He made it to the house and put Caroline down. They walked to the front door and opened it to enter. As they entered the house, they were greeted by another entity and another figure.

> *"John, I cannot let you leave with her."* The prominent figure said.
> *"Try and stop me, jackass,"* John responded.
> *"I am not sure you would like that outcome."*
> *"Move out of my way. I am taking her home."* John positioned himself between Caroline and the demon.

Abaddon

"I cannot hurt you, John, but I can take her life. Please don't make me do that. I don't want to do that."
"You would kill her?"
"I am Abaddon, the angel of death. My job is death for both heaven and hell. I was told she cannot leave. I cannot let her leave. I must follow my orders."
"Just move and let me get her back home."
"Please, we just want to get home," Caroline begged.
"There is little I can do about this. I am sorry. One of you can go back. So, John, I am sorry to say this. You two have a choice to make. Who stays, who goes?"

Caroline and John looked at each other, very confused. They both wanted to be home together and live their lives together, but they didn't know what to think of the situation in front of them now. They stood there momentarily, gazing into each other's eyes.

"You two need to decide and decide now," Abaddon said.
"I will not leave her here," John stated.
"John, no. You can't stay. He doesn't want you." Caroline said.

She did not want to stay but felt that John needed to go back home. She was doing her best to stay strong and not break down. She wanted nothing more than to return home with John and start their lives together. Her heart was breaking. She knew she could not go on without John in her life, but John would be able to move on and continue doing great things.

Abaddon

"Don't make me choose," Abaddon said impatiently.

John nodded at Caroline as if he were signaling her.

"Do you trust me, Caroline?"
"Yes, I do, John."
"What are you doing, you fool?" Abaddon questioned.

John held Caroline's hand. He closed his eyes and took a deep breath. He then headed for the stairs with Caroline.

"Boy, you don't know who I am and what I can do." Abaddon snapped.
"You cannot keep her here. She does not want to stay. I love her and will not allow you to keep her here."
"It is not your choice. Listen to me."

They were at the top of the stairs and heading down the hall to the room with the armoire. Abaddon was standing in front of them, blocking their way.

"Why won't you just let me leave?" Caroline screamed at him.
"I can't," Abaddon replied remorsefully.

John positioned himself between them, putting himself in front of Caroline and ensuring Caroline was protected.

"You have to do what Satan Says to do," Caroline said to him.

Abaddon

"Only to a point, dear child. You don't understand. I don't want to keep you here."
"Then let us by," John said.
"That is the one thing I cannot do. Back at your home, I am trapped. And if I let her leave, I will never be freed. I will be forever trapped. I will never be able to fulfill my job for God. I don't want either of you stuck here."
"What do you mean trapped?" Caroline asked in a soft, caring voice.
"If you don't want either of us to be stuck here, then let us go," John responded.
"Oh, Caroline, always so caring. Satan told me that he would release me of this curse my mother put on me. If you never leave hell. Once out of that body, I am stuck up there and will become my normal self. Then, I can fulfill my duties to God on judgment day. Then Satan will pay for everything he has done."

As they spoke, John was inching them closer to the room. Abaddon was slowly backing up, avoiding contact with them.

"I need you two to stay clear of my touch," Abaddon warned.
"And why is that?" John asked while inching forward.
"A single touch by me will cause you to stay here forever. And I don't want that to happen."

They were almost at that room. John knew they could rush around him and make it to the armoire. Then they would be home, and all this would be in the past. John grabbed

Abaddon

Caroline's hand again and dashed for the room. As they passed by Abaddon, he reached for John.

John quickly avoided being touched by him and watched Abaddon's hand swipe right by him. John ran over to the armoire and opened the door. He saw the red blanket inside. He grabbed the blanket and turned to hand it to Caroline. She was lying on the ground.

> *"Caroline. Take the blanket and get into the armoire. I'll help you if you want. Caroline?"*
> *"John. Somethings wrong."* She whispered as if she were falling asleep.

John quickly scooped her off the floor, placed the blanket in her arms, entered the old armoire, and closed the door.

> *"I got you. We are almost done."* John whispered to Caroline.

As he opened the door, he was met with disappointment. There in front of him was Abaddon. He stood there with a dumbfounded look on his face.

> *"Bring her to me, John,"* Abaddon said sadly.

John felt defeated. He had not been able to get Caroline out of hell, and he was also stuck there. As he held Caroline in his arms, he stepped out of the armoire.

> *"You did not fail my boy."*
> *"I didn't get her home."*
> *"The dead cannot go back."*

Abaddon

"The what?"
"The dead. Caroline is dead." **Abaddon said.**
"She's what?" John said in utter shock. *"But how? No. It can't be."*
"I am sorry, John."
"I don't understand."
"When you ran past me. I touched her."
"What do you mean? I dodged you."
"Yes, I know. But by dodging me, you opened her up. Before I could stop, she bumped into my hand."

John stood there in disbelief at what Abaddon was saying. His entire body started to tremble. He crouched down and rested Caroline on the floor. Her lifeless body lay there on the floor. Tears began to well up in John's eyes. He got weak in the knees; his body could no longer hold him up, and he dropped to the floor. John wept. He held her corpse against his body, tears falling from his face slowly and falling onto hers.

"John, I know you love her. I understand that you wanted a life with her..."
"You don't know shit, you murdering bastard." John interrupted Abaddon. *"You don't understand, you couldn't understand."* John snapped through the tears and guilt.
"You are right. I was not born with those emotions. But watching you has changed me. Seeing what my mother has commanded of the others has sickened me."
"I don't understand why you would not let us pass freely then."
"I have been commanded not to. My Mother..."

Abaddon

"Fuck your mother then. She should be lying dead on the floor. Who is your mother? Why me? Why all this?"
"She calls herself Lilith these days."

John looked up at Abaddon with anger in his eyes. The room began filling with a low fog covering the floor like someone had just turned on a fog machine. Something was coming—something or someone. The house started to shake—not like an earthquake, but as if mimicking the footsteps of some giant walking. Abaddon and John heard the front door slam shut.

"What did you say?" John asked slowly.
"I said she calls herself Lilith."
"You're telling me my ex-wife, Lilith, did all this?"
"Yes, that is right. Your ex-wife, my mother, wants to stop you from ever being happy." With remorse in his voice, Abaddon responded to John's question.
"But why? Why can't she leave me alone?"
"Since you and Mother got married, she has always seen you as capable of doing much more than you had. But she wanted you to go in a different direction than you felt pulled. She did not like how you would not do as she instructed. When you refused and continued trying to do good instead of trying to become famous, she left you and made a pact with Satan to do everything she could to stop you from being happy because she was mad at you. That is why Caroline left you the first time. Yes, you made mistakes and hurt her feelings. But you always managed somehow to keep her in your life. Mother was very displeased when she found that Caroline

Abaddon

had returned to your heart and life this last time. So, she set out to destroy your ability to be happy. She thought the only way would be to get Caroline out of your life, to make her leave you again. This is why we are here now. This is why I am now trapped inside a human body. Her son's body."

"Oh my God. You mean you are stuck in my... our son's body?" John asked.

"No, she has had another child. She had made a deal with Satan before all these events so she could have a second child, and she paid Satan for this child. She and Satan trapped me in this child's body. My older brother, your son, is unharmed and perfectly healthy. After meeting you here, I can tell you he is just like you. He is safe and healthy as well. I would do anything to protect him."

John noticed that as Abaddon spoke of his mother, he looked emotionless. However, as he spoke of John's son, John saw love in Abaddon's eyes.

John thought to himself, **"He cares about Samual. He loves him as his bother. How can this be? He said he was not made with those emotions."**

"I am sure you are wondering how I could feel care and love for your son, Samual. I am just as confused as you about that." Abaddon stated.
"I didn't say that."
"You didn't have to speak that. I can tell by the look on your face."
"Well, yes. I will admit I am confused."

Abaddon

"Listen to me, John. We are running out of time here for you. You need to get out of here before Satan makes it here, and you are lost forever. I need you to do something for me."
"Will it bring Caroline back?" John asked while wiping the tears from his face.
"No, I am the Angel of death. Once I touch a soul, it does not come back."
"Then fuck it and fuck you."
"It is for Samual's safety."
"Keep his name out of your fucking mouth." John snapped at Abaddon.
"I understand your position..." Abaddon began.
"You don't understand shit. You only understand death."
"I understand that if you don't do as I ask, Lilith will end up hurting him."

John thought about his son. He would do anything to protect that sweet, innocent boy of his. John remembered the love he saw in Abaddon's eyes when speaking of Samual. John looked at Caroline.

"What would you do?" He whispered as if she would respond.

John looked toward Abaddon again. He noticed Abaddon was handing him the blanket.

"Take it quickly, John, and go back home."

John ripped the blanket out of Abaddon's hands. He was glaring at Abaddon. He was almost free to go home with

Abaddon

Caroline, and now she is dead. John felt something rising in his soul. He had no idea what it was. But he had to ask Abaddon.

> *"What is it you want me to do,"* John said with little thought.
> *"I need you to get out of here now. But I also need you to kill Lilith, then find me in human form and kill me to reals me of this curse. NOW GO. He is coming."*

John took the blanket his mother had hand-knit and went into the armoire. As Abaddon shut the door, he saw a horrifying figure enter the room, but he merely caught a glimpse as he was busy looking at Caroline's dead body being engulfed in the fog that was moving in.

The figure and John looked at each other in the eyes for a moment. John's head was filled with millions of years of events in a flash. He saw the Garden of Eden, the fall of the angels into hell, Satan being cast out of heaven, and the millions of tortured souls that have inhabited hell.

Abaddon

Abaddon

Chapter 17

John stepped out of the armoire to find himself back in his house. The storm was still roaring outside. Father Johnson was in the room waiting for him. John was still full of fear and sadness from what he had just witnessed. He was sick to his stomach. He fell to the floor on his knees. Andrew ran to his side and kept from falling flat on his face.

"John, where is Caroline?" Andrew asked.
"There."
"But you found her. She was with you. Did you leave her there? What happened? I heard you, then your voice became muffled, and I could understand what you were saying."

John looked at him with tears in his eyes.

"She's gone, Andrew. I lost. I failed," John started crying.
"What do you mean gone?"
"He got her. She dead. Oh my God, she's dead." Was all John could get out of his mouth before breaking down. *"I have to kill her... I have to."*
"Kill who, John?"
"His mother, I have to free him."
"You're not making any sense, John. Kill who? And why?"
"His mother, then him."

"Whose mother? Who is 'he' that you have to kill? What are you talking about? What happened there?"
"The man."
"What, John? You aren't making any sense. I need you to calm down and tell me what happened," Andrew commanded, his voice filled with concern for his friend.

John was shaking uncontrollably. Andrew just sat on the ground and held John. John had broken down in tears, sobbing, and Andrew was trying to comfort him as best he could. He would try to talk to John about it later when he calmed down.

Andrew took John to a room and helped him into the bed. John was mumbling, but Andrew could not make heads or tails of what was being said. John's voice got softer and softer until he fell into a deep slumber. Once John was asleep, Andrew set up a place for him to sleep on the floor. Then, he left the room to get a drink. John was now asleep but talking in his sleep.

"Lilith..." John's voice whispered. *"Leave her alone... I love you, Caroline... I'm sorry."*

Andrew left John in the room and descended the stairs to the kitchen. The wind, a haunting symphony, continued to howl outside, its icy breath seeping through the cracks. As he reached the first floor, he caught sight of several shadowy figures, their forms distorted and indistinct, lurking at the front door windows and in the yard. The unmistakable signs of an evil presence. Andrew knew he would need John's help to confront this. But for now, he had to wait for John to regain

Abaddon

his clarity. Ignoring the figures, he made his way to the kitchen, the only safe haven in the house, to strategize.

Andrew swiftly grabbed his bag and began pulling out the tools and supplies he and John needed to battle this situation and clear the house.

Several days passed, and John slept. Andrew stayed at the house until John was better. Throughout each day and night, Andrew would make time to pray over John and the house. He noticed that as he continued to do this, fewer and fewer demons approached the house. On the third day, John awoke from his slumber. Andrew was sleeping on the floor and started to wake up himself.

"You're finally awake, my friend." Andrew greeted him.
"Yes. How long have I been asleep?" John asked.
"It's been about three days."
"Three days?" John repeated as he rubbed the sleep out of his eyes. *"I need to get shit done."*
"Calm down, we have plenty of time. I have been working on things myself while you were out."
Andrew assured John as they were getting up for their sleep.

The two men got ready for their day separately. They were both ready for breakfast and to start the day. John was still remembering the images that were burned into his mind when leaving hell. As if he had been there watching those events unfold in person.

They went to the café to grab some food. The sun was out. There was a cool breeze and not a cloud in sight. It was already getting warm out, so the breeze was needed.

Abaddon

The men talked about the events they had just experienced, recapping everything almost step by step while they sat in the corner booth of the café.

"And then looked into his eyes as he came into the room. I saw things, Andrew. I saw them as if they were my memories. Then Abaddon shut the door. Then I opened it again, and I saw you."
"What did you say his name was?"
"Abaddon. Why?"
"So, you mean to tell me that you were talking to the angel of death?"
"I guess. You're the God guy, not me."
"Ok, John, Listen to me. The man you saw entering the room while you were leaving was Satan. So, count your blessings you got out of there."
"That was the ruler of hell coming after me?" John said while chuckling.
"I know you don't believe in all this, so thank you for humoring me here."
"How do you know all of this? I don't remember any of this from the Bible."
"Well, remember two things. I have been there, and God speaks to me." Andrew responded.
"Yes, I almost forgot, you're a priest. Why wouldn't God talk to you about things like what hell looks like."
"No, John, I don't think you understand. God talks to me like you, and I are talking. It is audible in my head."
"So, you hear voices in your head?"

Abaddon

"Not like you are suggesting. But yes." Andrew explained. *"He is talking to me right now. He says that you have some work to do to help him."*
"Don't we all have to do work for God? Like, spread the gospel?" John said mockingly.
"I appreciate a good joke as much as you do. But he is telling me that you must do what Abaddon asked of you."
"Listen, Andrew, I am not into games. And I'm still not sure what I just saw. Hell, you could have put something in the Tea and whatever you made me drink for all I know."
"This is unusual for sure. God is telling me that you have only a twenty-dollar bill in your wallet and three-quarters in your pocket."
"Oh, so it is magic time. Yes, I have a twenty in my wallet." He stated while shaking his head. He then reached into his pocket to pull the coins out. *"How the fuck did you know?"* He said as he looked at the three shiny quarters.
"God needs you to listen to me since you have not been listening to him."

John drank his coffee, thinking of what Andrew had just said. He wanted to believe, but he couldn't. Every time he followed the Lord or believed in Him, his life seemed to fall apart. He took a deep breath.

"Okay, Andrew. You win. Let's do this. What next."
"God is saying you need to free Abaddon."
John was apprehensive but asked, *"Okay, so you are saying God wants me to kill? And I am not being a*

dick here. Abaddon said he needed me to kill 'Lilith,' my ex-wife."
"He needs you to free Abaddon. And I am guessing if that is the only way to do it, then yes."
"Well, that is not all he said I needed to do."
"What do you mean? What else did he say?"
"I need to find him and kill his human self."
"Then, yes. You need to do that."
"When? How?"
"We will work a plan tonight."

That evening, they sat at the kitchen table devising a plan. It was a simple plan. John would go to Lilith's place and simply stab her or whatever it would take to end her life. Then, they would start looking for Abaddon and do the same thing.

"I don't even know where she lives anymore," John stated in frustration.
"She has your son. How do you not know where she lives?"
"She took him away from me. I haven't been able to see him for two years."
"Grab a pen and paper."

A pad of paper and a pen were on the table. John picked them up and was ready to write.

"900... West Main St... Here in town... no, I'm sorry. She lives downtown." Andrew slowly spoke as if he was relaying a message.

Abaddon

John wrote the address down as Andrew said it. He looked at the address. He knew this place. His son lived only 30 Minutes away, and John didn't even know this. He felt like the worst father ever. But in that moment, a glimmer of hope sparked within him. They had their little plan; John was ready, more than ever, to do this.

Abaddon

Chapter 18

The sun had set, and the moon shone in the clear sky. John sat outside the apartment building his ex-wife lived in. He saw that she had a light on through the living room window. He had earlier seen his son leave with his grandparents. He was about to get out of the car with the knife in hand when he noticed the light go off in the apartment. He was nervous; he was not a killer, yet here he was, ready to kill his ex-wife. Moments later, he saw Lilith exit the front door of the building. She walked around the corner of the building and down the street. Ironically, she looked as though she belonged on the streets with the attire she had on.

John did not follow her. He went to her unit and figured he would hide and wait for her to return. When he got there, the door was unlocked. He constantly looked over his shoulder to ensure no one followed or saw him. He quickly and quietly entered Lilith's apartment. There was not any light coming in from the night sky, so John pulled his phone out of his pants pocket and turned the flashlight on so he could see where he was going. He crept around the apartment, trying to find a place to hide, but her apartment was so small and sparsely decorated he was having trouble finding a spot. He came across her a door to a room. It had locks keeping anyone out of it. He noticed a light glowing from under the door.

Across from it was her room. John entered her bedroom. It fit a chest of drawers, her bed, two nightstands, and a mirror standing in the corner. As he looked around the room, he saw a very old-looking book on the nightstand. He walked over to it so he could see what it was. As he approached it, he noticed a silver bowl next to it full of a dark red liquid. The book was open as if someone had been reading it earlier, put it down, and did not want to lose their spot.

He dipped his finger in the bowl and rubbed the liquid between his fingers. It was a thick red substance—it was blood. He started to examine the book, filled with demonic pictures and incantations. He began to read the Paige's the book was open to. He was shocked by what he was reading. It appeared to him to be instructions on how to conjure up demons and have control over them to attack another human. He heard the front door open and close; then, he heard the locks being locked.

He quickly looked around in a panic. The closet was closest to him, so he hid in it. He heard her footsteps getting closer to the room. She came into the room and started getting undressed. As he avoided watching her, he noticed someone sleeping in the closet. There was a pillow and blanket on the floor. She opened the closet door; he looked up, but she did not see him behind the clothing. She grabbed her black robe and put it on but did not cover herself by closing it. He noticed several bite marks on her chest and abdomen. They all looked like old scars, except one was still bleeding.

As she walked out of the room, she grabbed her keys. It sounded like she went to the door across from her room and unlocked the door. John heard the door open and then shut. He headed that way. He pulled the knife out of the inside pocket of his jacket and slowly walked into the other room after her.

She had candles burning and was sitting in the middle of them on the floor chanting. Her eyes were closed. Now was his chance. He crept up on her from behind.

Abaddon

As if something warned her of his presence, she spun around and grabbed his arm with the knife in it. She stood up; her eyes were black as night and void of life, void of her. Lilith grabbed John by the throat and picked him up by one arm, then threw him across the room. When he hit the wall, he dropped the knife.

"You dumb son of a bitch. How dare you disrupt me like that." Lilith growled. *"What did you think you could do? Come into my house and kill me. You cannot get rid of me, John. I will be here till the day you die."*

John was scrambling to get back up and get the knife. Within the blink of an eye, Lilith was in front of him as if she were moving at the speed of light. She grabbed him again by the neck and threw John to the ground. He landed right by the knife. He quickly grabbed it, then rolled to his back just as Lilith jumped on him. He thrust the blade into her stomach and twisted it to ensure that he inflicted as much damage as possible with it.

Lilith let out a gasp as the blade entered her body. Her body went limp, and she fell to the ground. As he pulled the knife from her body, her blood began to pour out of her. It was black as crude oil.

John heard an eerie voice whisper, *"Thank you. I am almost free."*

John felt horrible about what he had just done. He had never killed a person before. He was breathing heavily and shaking; he felt like he had to leave quickly. He felt sick to his stomach and needed to get back home.

Abaddon

John was pulling into the driveway and still feeling nauseous. He parked the car and walked himself into the house. His shirt was covered in Lilith's blood; he was still shaking. He moved quickly to the stairs he needed to get the shirt off.

"John, is that you?" Andrew shouted from the kitchen.
"Yes, it's me. I did it. I need to get this shirt off of me." John's voice was still shaking.
"I think I know where this Abaddon character is."
"We can talk about that when I come back down."

John went to his room to change shirts. He took the blood-soaked shirt off to throw on an old concert t-shirt and headed back downstairs to the kitchen. Andrew was sitting at the table with a notepad, reading over the information he had gathered. His Bible lay open on the table next to the notepad.

"So, Andrew, you claim to know where I can find this Abaddon guy possibly. Where?"
"It appears he works at a bar downtown."
"What bar?"
"You need to relax. We will find him and do what we need to so he can be freed."

The two men sat down, and John tried to relax more. He calmed down, and the nauseous feeling subsided. They chatted about life and their pasts, getting to know each other better. Lilith, God, or Abaddon were never brought up in the discussion.

Abaddon

"Tell me more about why Caroline left you the first time."

"Oh boy. Let's say I messed up and hurt her feelings."

"You didn't cheat on her, did you?"

"No, nothing like that."

"Tell me then. You always say you will not make that mistake again; what mistake?"

"I wasn't attentive to her wants and needs." John reluctantly said. *"She was everything to me. She was not perfect, but she was perfect to me. I was the happiest I had ever been when talking to her or being around her. I would have done anything and everything to keep her in my life and 'keep' her happy. She was the most important thing in the world to me. But I missed some signs or signals. She felt that I was focused only on me. I just messed up. That is why I hung onto every word she would say when she came back into my life. So that I never missed a single thing. In a nutshell, she was going through some things in her life. And I came across as dismissive toward those things and her. She tired of dealing with my dismissive attitude and called it off."*

"So, you didn't pay attention to her emotional needs?"

"I thought I was, but no."

"But you loved her."

"With all my being. Even though she is gone, I still love her. And miss her."

"What was it about her?"

"Everything. The way she helped me, completed my thoughts, looked at me. Her laugh, her smile, her eyes. Her strength, her independence. The way she

keeps pushing forward. And so much more." John replied with tears in his eyes.
"You really loved her, didn't you?"
"More than anything."
"Let me ask you this. What is love to you?"
"To quote, I believe it was Socrates, and I am going to butcher it, I am sure. He explained love as a desire." John started.
"What do you mean?" Andrew asked.
"Does a strong man want to be strong? Does a wealthy man want to be wealthy?"
"No, they already are."
"No, they do want to be those things. They desire it daily. So, they do what it takes to keep it. That is love. They desire to have tomorrow what they have today. That was me with Caroline. I desired her in my life today, tomorrow, and next. That, to me, is love."
"And your other wife, Lilith?"
"No. When she left me, it hurt, but I got over that. When Caroline left me the first time. There was a void, a hole, in me. I felt empty. Like a part of me was missing."
"I still don't understand what you did wrong."
"I did not always pay attention to her needs and emotions. I am not sure I can ever forgive myself for that." John said with a lot of regret and remorse in his voice. *"I wasn't there for her when I needed to be… when she needed me to be. I never asked the proper questions. She always seemed to have everything in her life under control, even though she said she didn't. I didn't ask her the right questions. I didn't pay attention. I focused too much on myself. I didn't focus on her enough…"* John started to tear up.

Abaddon

John began repeating himself softly. He was distraught by this immense loss. He began to tremble. His speech started to shake. The regret weighed heavy on his heart and soul. He had always been able to 'fix' things in his life, but he saw no way to fix this. There was no way for him to get forgiveness from her for hurting her that way.

> *"I understand, I think. You regret not fully investing yourself in the relationship. You regret not paying attention to her needs."* Andrew said while patting John on the hand.
> John replied softly through his tears, *"Yes. But I was fully invested in the relationship. I did not pay enough attention to her needs, which ripped me apart. I was even given a second chance, which was taken away."*

John was showing his emotions at this point. He was heartbroken by the turn of events. He had just witnessed the love of his life slip through his hands again. This time, with no chance of returning to him. The sorrow and guilt he felt were immense. He was mourning the loss of her as a partner and her life. He started to tear up just thinking of her. He longed to hold Caroline again, to kiss her one more time. She always had a way of igniting his soul. When she was around, he felt unstoppable, almost untouchable.

John was left to muster up this drive alone and had to find courage again. He knew he could do this; it was easier with Caroline.

> *"John, we need to get going."*
> *"Go where?"* John asked.
> *"To find Abaddon."*

Abaddon

"You said you found him."
"Yes, I did. We want to confirm this."
"I don't get it, but okay."

Andrew and John began their drive to the downtown area over the bar, which he believed to be Abaddon's place of employment. As they pulled up to the bar, John noticed it was just a short distance from Lilith's apartment. It was in an underdeveloped part of town, but it appeared to be an upper-class establishment. The bar was dimly lit and filled with smoke and noise.

"It looked a lot nicer from the outside," Andrew observed.
"Not your typical hang-out spot, a father." John joked.
"Not anymore, not anymore."

As they walked around the bar, John noticed the bartender and pointed him out to Andrew.

"That's him, Andrew; that is Abaddon. That is the son of a bitch that killed Caroline."

John instantly felt the pain and anger well up in him as he looked at Abaddon behind the bar, smiling. The bar was swarming with patrons, making it hard to move around.

"He knows who you are, so try to stay out of sight, John. Just keep a low profile."

As Andrew advised, John did his best to stay out of sight to avoid being recognized. Andrew walked toward the

Abaddon

bar. With the large crowd and neon glowing throughout the bar, added to the haze of smoke wafting through the building, John figured it would be easy to keep hidden. John watched, wondering what Andrew would do once he got the bar. As Andrew approached the bar, he appeared to be very calm. Andrew leaned in, caught Abaddon's eye, and nodded, lifting his hand to hold two fingers in the air. Abaddon nodded back, grabbed two glasses, then a bottle from the top shelf, poured two glasses of bourbon, and handed them over to Andrew; they appeared to exchange a few words; then Andrew paid for the drinks and headed back toward John.

> *"Here you go, John. Drink up, and let's get out of here," Andrew said* as he handed the glass to John and then downed the drink.
> *"What happened?"*
> *"Just finish the drink so we can get out here."*
> *"Damn, never seen a priest encourage drinking as much as you are now."*
> *"Funny, just hurry up. We need to go."*
> *"Alrighty,"* John responded.

John finished his drink quickly, and they headed out the door. As they reached the door, they heard a scream behind them. A fight was breaking out and spreading rapidly across the establishment. John saw a man pull out a knife and stab a few other patrons. Abaddon rushed toward the man to break the fight up, and then the man slashed the blade across the air to ward off Abaddon. Instead of scaring him away, Abaddon fearlessly advanced. As Abaddon went to grab the man to subdue him, the knife sliced through the air one last time, striking Abaddon and delivering a deep gash to Abaddon's face.

Abaddon

Abaddon grinned as the blood from the cut rolled down his face. It was as if he enjoyed being attacked, as if it made him excited to be in battle. Like an animal, Abaddon instantly pounced on the man, disarming him with the knife and dismantling his body. Several other people joined in by trying to jump Abaddon, kicking and punching him; this seemed to fuel him and assist him. The crowd went wild like they were at a stadium watching their favorite team winning an MMA match.

The crowd was cheering him on. It was quite a spectacle to watch Abaddon in action, fending off each attacker like they were nothing but flies being swatted away. The faces of the people in the crowd were contorting; their eyes were turning black or red. They appeared to hunger for the blood to be spilled feverishly. The people in the front seemed to enjoy having blood splatter across their faces.

Standing victorious, Abaddon scanned the crowd, looking at his fans, all cheering for him. He looked directly at John and Andrew; his eyes locked on John. He stared at John long enough for John to notice. John was now seen; Abaddon looked pleased to see him. It was not a pleasant look he was giving John. It was very unsettling to John the way he was looking at him, as if he wanted to cause John harm, possibly dismembering John next.

"Let's go, John," Andrew said as he grabbed John's arm and pulled him to the door.

John reluctantly nodded his head in agreeance and followed Andrew out the door. Leaving Abaddon standing there in the bar over his slain victims. John could get over what he had just witnessed and the people cheering Abaddon

Abaddon

on. He was killing those men. He had ripped them apart piece by piece.

John and Andrew left the establishment and headed to Andrew's car. In disbelief, John was shaken by what he had just witnessed and sat in the car. Andrew appeared unfazed.

Abaddon

Abaddon

Chapter 19

The neon lights from the bar illuminated the inside of the car. The two men sat outside the bar, waiting for Abaddon to leave. They planned to wait for Abaddon to leave work, follow him away from the people and the crowd, and John would free him. They needed to do this in private, with no witnesses.

For some reason, John was stressing out about this situation as if he were planning the execution of a public figure. He nervously tapped his hand on his knee rhythmically while bouncing his leg to a faster beat. From the driver's seat, Andrew looked at John and noticed his current state.

"Why are you so nervous, John? He wants you to do this. He asked you too."
"What if it's a trick? You sa... the bib... I thought the devil was a trickster?"
"That was a demon, an angel. Both. Not Satan."
"What the hell is the difference, Andrew? This thing, this person. It's crazy. Did you see the way he killed that man with the knife? He even got cut and wasn't even phased by it."
"No, he wasn..."
"We need to leave. Leave now, Andrew." John interrupted.
"What?" Andrew was shocked by this.
"Something wasn't right in there. We just need to go home."
"He should be off soon. Let's wait. Stick to the plan."

"No, we need to leave. He is going to see us."
"How?"
"This car."
"What's wrong with this car? He's not going to see it."
John looked at Andrew, *"Who still drives a 1986 Oldsmobile? It looks like something from an old cop show. It's like we are staking the place out or something. Can we just leave, for fucks sake?"*
"I don't understand this change, John."
"The look he gave me. That look in his eyes. He didn't want me to kill him. He looked like he wanted to fight me or kill me or both. I don't feel safe about this. Call it a gut feeling or whatever. Just start the fucking car and drive."

Andrew started the car.

"Okay, maybe you're right. We should go now."

As he put the car in drive, a giant demon dropped onto the hood. Half its face had been burned off, and the gallons of its feet dug into the car's hood. Its wings engulfed the entire view out of the windshield.
It was crouching down and peering into the car at John.

"You think you can stop me by killing Abaddon's host body? You think you can free him and stop me, John?"
"Be gone, demon," Andrew shouted.
"That is cute priest. I am no mere demon. You are trying to fuck with the 'demon' here."

Abaddon

"You have no power over us. God our father…"
"Shut up, priest. I am here for John. He killed my Lilith. I know what you are trying to do, little boy."

Andrew slowly exited the car, and John sat frozen in his seat. The fear of this monster staring down at John was paralyzing, and the stench that filled the inside of the car was unbearable. The grotesque smell was getting worse in the car; it was thick and beginning to cause John trouble breathing. It was like the smell of rotting flesh and garbage.

"I said, be gone, Satan," Andrew announced. Again sternly.
"What the fuck… Satan?" John whispered in fear.
"Leave the human be," Andrew announced.

Outside, a blindingly bright light, a bright white light, shone. John covered his eyes to protect them. John watched as Satan slowly turned his head toward Andrew. When John looked at Andrew, he saw that his body was producing this light. He noticed Andrew had large, beautiful white wings that seemed to stretch out forever. He was no longer in his black slacks, which John had become accustomed to seeing him in, but a long white robe with a gold sash as a belt. His hair was shoulder length and brown instead of balding and grey.

"I command you, Satan, to leave this man now. Leave this earth never to come back."
"Well, well, well. Who might this be? Is this my little brother Cherubim?" Satan questioned as he began to chuckle.
"Yes, brother, it is. Now, do as I have stated. Or

else."
"Or else what, little one? Your father will come reprimand me?" Mockingly, Satan replied.
"You know what will happen," Cherubim replied.
"And it is not that time."
"Fuck you, and fuck your Father, your God."

Satan then morphed into a humanoid, still dawning large black reptilian wings. He stepped off the car toward Cherubim, breathing heavily out of anger.

"I haven't seen or heard from Him in thousands of years. What makes you think He will do anything to me? I have taken many of these humans, and he hasn't done a thing."
"I was not speaking of God. I was speaking about me." Cherubim stated firmly.
Satan began to laugh, *"You? You, little brother? I am not afraid of you. I fear nothing or anything."*
"Except Abaddon. And our Father God."

This statement angered him. His large black wings extended instantly, much larger than Cherubim's. He towered over Cherubim.

"Get out of here, John," Cherubim shouted.

Satan quickly grabbed Cherubim by the neck, and in the blink of an eye, he flew off into the night sky. John was left sitting alone in the passenger seat of the car. He quickly Jumped over to the driver's seat and attempted to start the vehicle. The engine would not turn over; only the starter motor was cranking. John looked at the hood of the car; the

Abaddon

damage was gone. He could smell the fuel from flooding the engine with the number of attempts he made to start the car. He knew the car was not going to start at this point. He got out of the car and began his journey home. There was still no site of Satan or Andrew. He walked off into the night, wondering what had happened to Andrew. Was this man really an angel? He had so many questions that were not answered. Riddled with fear and confusion, he walked toward his house, hoping to find answers or Andrew there.

      He became sad as he entered the cold, dark, silent house. There was no Caroline to greet him, no answers, just confusion and emptiness. He went up to the room and began packing a
bag. The house felt like it was no longer breathing and was now void of life. The flooring hardly seemed to creek as he walked the halls or the rooms. He grabbed his bag, which was now full, and started turning off lights and closing the house, ready to leave. That night, there was no storm, rain, or lightning; it was a clear, dark sky with nothing but the full moon and stars to light one way. John had his bag, turned, and gave the house one last good look, then closed the front door and started walking down the driveway away from the house.

Abaddon

Chapter 20

"It's been an eternity, or so it seems, and there's no trace of John. It's as if he's been swallowed by the earth. I've searched all his usual spots, and not a single person has seen him." Abaddon's voice trembled with concern, the puzzle of John's sudden absence weighing heavily on his mind, the doubt evident in his words.
"So, he just up and disappeared? Like, without a trace? As the angel of death, I thought you could see every soul and know where it is." Paige question.
"Consider this a warning to all of what is to come and why it is going to happen differently than the way they have read or consider this a 'help wanted' ad. Possibly, I am hoping he is out there and will read your writings. That is my true hope."
"So, you are doing all this as a 'help wanted' sign?"
"Truly? Yes, I am hopeful that he will see this, as I stated, and find me. I am out of options and have no clue when God will call on me again. I am desperate, Paige. I don't know what else to do currently."

Paige sat on the couch, thinking over the story she had just spent hours listening to—the words Abaddon spoke. She could not understand it all, but then again, she never understood the Bible either.

Abaddon

"I know it is late, Paige. Would you like another drink?" Abaddon politely asked.
"Yes, please. That would be splendid." She kindly accepted. *"I have to ask."*
"Yes."
"This house."
"This is John's house, isn't it?"
"Not anymore. After he disappeared, the house went up for auction. So, I bought it."
"But it was the house he and Caroline were working on in your story?"
"Yes, it is."
"And that priest. Andrew right or Father Johnson?"
"Yes, what about him?"
"Was he another angel? Or was that like some angelic possession thing that happened the night they went to the bar you were working at?"

Abaddon started to chuckle. He poured Paige another cup of coffee from the pot on the table. He went and poured himself another drink.

"Ahh, yes, my dear brother Cherubim, or Andrew as you call him. He is, in fact, an angel."
"Was he sent from God to help John?"
"Yes, he was. God sent him to protect John."
Paige was packing her belongings, *"Is that everything you had to say?"* She asked.
"Was that not enough for you?" Abaddon responded.
"It's not that. It's getting late. The storm seems to be passing. I should get going and start on this writing for you."

Abaddon

"I understand; yes, it is getting late. You should get heading home. If I think of any other details, I will reach out."
"You do have my contact information, and I do have other questions."
"Like what?"
"I want to know more about John."
"We can discuss those later. I wish you safe travels..."

Abaddon sat there in his chair with a stunned look on his face. His glass slipped out of his hand and shattered on the wooden floor. He started to slump over in his chair. A blade sticking out of his abdomen.

"Abaddon?" Paige spoke with concern in her voice.
"Abaddon, are you ok?"
"I hope this releases you," John stated.
Abaddon started to smile, *"Yes, my boy. Thank you. My soul can now be free."* Abaddon looked down at his abdomen to see a blade sticking out of him.
Paige was in shock, *"Holy shit! You killed him."* She said as she looked at the sword blade from Abaddon's abdomen.
"It's okay, Paige. This is what I needed. John, you came back. You did not leave me or this world stranded."
"I only did what he asked of me." Responded to Paige
"Thank you, my friend." Those were the last words he spoke as a human.

Paige stood in the living room in shock. She looked at John to ensure he was not coming after her next. She was frozen in her own skin, and a look of terror covered her face. She did not know if she should scream, run, or welcome the man, so she stood there, not making a sound or movement. She stared at the man behind the chair. He did not look like the man she had imagined when Abaddon talked about him. He looked as if he had not eaten in days. His hair was long and uncombed. He looked tired as if he had not had a warm meal or slept well in weeks.

  The room was filled with a blinding white light as Abaddon's essence left his human body. It did not ascend upward or sink into the earth. It walked slowly toward the house's entry and then exited. Before the light left the room, two other people entered. Paige and John stood next to each other, watching.

  "John?" A soft voice spoke.

  John's eyes lit up. He knew that voice. His heart skipped a beat as he heard it. Was he dreaming? Was this real?

  Shocked, he answered, "Caroline? Is that you?"
"John." She answered excitedly.

  When their eyes connected, bystanders could have felt the love between them. Due to their deep love for each other, the light became brighter. They went to each other. John embraced Caroline so tight as to never let her go. John kissed her passionately.

  "I thought I had lost you."
"He sent me back," Caroline said lovingly.

Abaddon

"I love you so much and never want to lose you again."
"I'm not going anywhere, John." She reassured him.
"I am so sorry I let this happen to you." He said to Caroline as the tears fell down his cheek.
"It's okay, it's not your fault. God gave us another chance."
"Another chance?"
"He told me I could come back to you if you freed Abaddon for him. And you did, Not knowing that I would come back. You did it anyway."
"I would have done it sooner if I had known this."
"But you didn't, and you freed him anyway. That is what matters. Your selfless act."
"But you can still love me even knowing I just killed two people?"
"I will always love you, John. I will always stand by you."
"Andrew, is that you?" John asked inquisitively.
"Cherubim is actually the name, but yes." He replied.
"Thank you for bringing her back."
"I was just a guide. This is all God's doing."

They continued to hold each other as Paige stood there in observance. Even she felt and saw the overwhelming love they had for each other. She could see it all over John's face. Paige slowly collected her belongings and slipped out of the room.

John and Caroline held hands tightly as they walked to the door to leave the house and the nightmare they had lived in behind. As they reached the door, John opened it to usher Caroline out to the garage where his car was Parked. He

Abaddon

turned his head one last time toward the living room. Abaddon's body had ceased to move anymore. His head fell forward. His arm holding the drink merely went limp and hung to the side of his chair.

Outro

Paige sat on her computer and typed Abaddon's story. This time, she would not post it on her blog but would write her first book.

"I decided to write this story for Abaddon even though John returned to free him. It is no longer a 'help wanted' sign or a warning. It is a story of intense love that nothing could ever break it.

I hope the broken-hearted or those in love will cherish their partner and continue working on that love. Never let it grow weak; never let it go. I have never felt a love as strong as John had for Caroline and her for him. I want that kind of love in my life to be reciprocated. One day, this dream might come true for me. I know this is not my usual writing, to write about love.

Usually, I write about events on my blog that have to do with demonic possessions or sightings. But I was compelled by Abaddon's and John's stories, and I had to share the events I was told with you. This world can be a cold, dark, and cruel place. Finding love and keeping it alive is difficult. But it is possible to keep it alive regardless of the circumstances. This man, John, went to hell to prove his love for Caroline even after she had left him. Their relationship was just in the beginning phases, yet he loved her so deeply he put his own life in danger for her. Not many people would do that.

Abaddon

  It takes a strong person to admit his mistakes and work on correcting them. Growing as individuals is one of the most important things we can do. But having that type of insight into yourself and the ability to self-reflect is a blessing; it is almost a superpower.
  Being willing and able to have that level of self-reflection is genuinely glorious. To put yourself through 'hell' by looking at your past, admit your flaws, and then work on fixing them. Doing that for yourself and the other person you love makes you unstoppable.
  Love has no limits. It endures, outlasts anything, and has no end or fading hope. It can also refer to unconditional love, which is affection without limitations or conditions. 1 Corinthians 13:7-8 says, "Love knows no limit to its endurance, no end to its trust, no fading of its hope; it can outlast anything." I hope that you all can see that John loved Caroline. He had no reservations or limits with his love for her. He was willing to do anything and everything for her to prove his love to her. Too often, we react too quickly to people's words and don't give them the time to show us their feelings within their actions. Don't ignore the actions and efforts. You never know what you might be missing out on. They could be your answer."

  Paige took a sip from the glass of wine on her desk. She looked at the final words she had typed and was pleased with what she had written. She saved her document and uploaded it to the site to be published. She closed her laptop, turned off the lights in her house, and then turned in for the night.
  Abaddon stood outside across the street from her house, watching her work on his story and being pleased to

Abaddon

see her complete it. As she turned off the lights, he turned and walked away into the night and faded away.

Abaddon

Acknowledgment

    I hope we have all experienced love; I am sure most of us have experienced loss or the loss of that love. The pain of loss is insurmountable; it is unbelievable. Some may push that pain below and move on with their lives as if nothing happened. Others take time to wallow in their self-pity. Others need to take their time and process what just happened. Few of us are given a task and another chance at love with that particular person. But regardless, each of us must push forward as we never know what will happen next in our lives. Regardless of what has happened in our lives, we need to keep moving forward.

    I want to take this time to thank my kids for their love, my friends, my dear friends. I appreciate your support for reading these pages as I continued to write them and make the book grow, for reviewing my changes, and for giving me feedback. Thank you for supporting me and my dream of writing more fictional novels.

    Jennifer, JJ, thank you so much for creating the cover. You captured a feeling of this story I could never have imagined. I have been mulling over all of your feedback and questions about this story, and I hope I have been able to address all of them in this creation. Your assistance on this project has been invaluable to me. All of your insightful words have helped me grow, not only as a writer but also as a person. And that is a gift that will last me a lifetime.

    To everyone reading this, thank you for supporting me and my endeavor here. Your support does not go unseen

Abaddon

or unknown. I am profoundly humbled and grateful to you. I hope you have enjoyed this book. Feel free to leave a review on Amazon.